Lee Avarice paced on the plush, cream carpet, checking his watch again. The red colon blinked another miserable second. In some vain attempt to calm his nerves, he closed his eyes and breathed deep.

When he opened them, a gold letter opener caught his reflection. Lee picked it up and tilted his head to the left. The nick from his morning shave was still noticeable. He set the tool back on the desk and patted the sides of his hair. His botched haircut made him look like an aged Harry Potter in a windstorm. *Does it matter how presentable I appear?*

The knock came, firm and loud. Confident.

He's here. Lee straightened his glasses and cleared his throat. "Come in." *Maybe I should greet him.* He started to walk to the door, but then glanced back at his cherry-wood desk and slid behind it. A location of power. *Should I sit? No, I'll stand.*

The door opened.

His heart skipped.

A barrel of a gun stared him in the face.

"Hello, Lee."

"What's the meaning of this?" He swallowed hard and lifted his gaze from the gun to the would-be-shooter.

"I think you know." The gloved-hand cocked the trigger.

Sweat dripped from his forehead into his eyes. *What have I done? Think.* Useless information flowed through his mind, nothing worthy of this moment. Not that he hadn't made enemies. With hands raised, he walked around the front of the desk. "What's this about?"

No answer.

Praise for Kimberlee R. Mendoza

"Mendoza writes with the mind of a chess champion. She's always at least three moves ahead of her reader"
~*Paul McShane (Good News, Etc.)*

Confessions of a Con Man

by

Kimberlee R. Mendoza

Confessions of a Con Man

Cover Art by *Kimberlee R. Mendoza*

The Wild Rose Press, Inc.
PO Box 708
Adams Basin, NY 14410-0708
Visit us at www.thewildrosepress.com

Publishing History
First Mainstream Mystery Edition, 2016
Print ISBN 978-1-5092-0957-6
Digital ISBN 978-1-5092-0958-3

Published in the United States of America

Dedication

To Kip Kiplinger
and the family legacy he leaves behind

Chapter One

Lee Avarice paced on the plush, cream carpet, checking his watch again. The red colon blinked another miserable second. In some vain attempt to calm his nerves, he closed his eyes and breathed deep.

When he opened them, a gold letter opener caught his reflection. Lee picked it up and tilted his head to the left. The nick from his morning shave was still noticeable. He set the tool back on the desk and patted the sides of his hair. His botched haircut made him look like an aged Harry Potter in a windstorm. *Does it matter how presentable I appear?*

The knock came, firm and loud. Confident.

He's here. Lee straightened his glasses and cleared his throat. "Come in." *Maybe I should greet him.* He started to walk to the door, but then glanced back at his cherry-wood desk and slid behind it. A location of power. *Should I sit? No, I'll stand.*

The door opened.

His heart skipped.

A barrel of a gun stared him in the face.

"Hello, Lee."

"What's the meaning of this?" He swallowed hard and lifted his gaze from the gun to the would-be-shooter.

"I think you know." The gloved-hand cocked the trigger.

Sweat dripped from his forehead into his eyes. *What have I done? Think.* Useless information flowed through his mind, nothing worthy of this moment. Not that he hadn't made enemies. With hands raised, he walked around the front of the desk. "What's this about?"

No answer.

"I'm sure we can fix whatever it is." His knees buckled underneath him. "Please." He clasped his hands in front of him. "Please, I don't deserve to die."

"Say good-bye, Mr. Avarice."

"I could pay you."

The gun cocked.

Lee's throat tightened. His head swam. "Whatever it is, I can fix it." A deafening bang sounded. Warm blood. Then darkness.

Chapter Two

Stan Heller sat at the kitchen counter with an open newspaper and a lukewarm cup of coffee. A noise at the door drew his focus from the sports page. His dad, George was home. And from what Stan detected from his father's posture, it was from a long shift.

"Rough night?"

"You could say that." George took off his suit jacket, unbuckled his shoulder holster, and laid both on the counter. "I'm getting too old for this."

"One more year and you can retire, Dad." Stan crossed to the microwave and popped his mug inside to reheat. "At least you're not in my shoes. The captain made me help out on three different cases. I wish he'd assign me to just one."

George laughed. "The captain is feeling you out. He knows you're one of the best."

"Can't tell by the way he treats me. I have a perfect record so far. After all, look at my bloodline." He nudged his father's arm with his elbow. "Three generations of the best detectives God could create."

"It's grade-A DNA."

His dad and he were close. The old man always said, "Looking at Stan was like staring into a mirror thirty years ago." Brown hair, green eyes, and a chiseled chin that expressed determination and fortitude. With the exception of his dad's speckled gray hair and a few wrinkles, they were identical in every way.

Stan withdrew his coffee and sipped, then yanked it back. "Owe! A bit too hot."

George reached for Stan's discarded newspaper. "You home for the night?"

"No, I'm pulling a double."

"You say you're too old for this, but realistically, you're ridiculous."

His dad winked and punched the button on the answering machine. Stan's girlfriend, Melissa's voice filtered through the air. "Hey, honey. Hate to bother you, but if you have a moment, can you call me? I have a few questions. Thanks. Love you."

"Don't keep her waiting. Pretty girls don't like that."

Stan rolled his eyes. His dad—cop? No, relentless matchmaker. "You're incorrigible, you know that old man."

"Why? Because I want my son to have good dating manners?"

Stan leaned across the counter on his elbows, staring his father in the eye. "No, because underneath that advice is a reminder to propose marriage before you're sixty."

With a fake gasp, George sat back. "Don't be absurd. I would never push for my son to finally settle down and provide me with some grandchildren before I die. Absurd."

"You remind me almost every day." Stan stood back and set his cup in the empty sink.

"Can I help it if I want my son to be happy?"

"You're so obvious, Dad. This is about *your*

happiness. Like you just said. It's about *you* wanting grandchildren."

"So what if I do?" His dad's cell phone vibrated on the counter, but he didn't pick it up.

With a smirk, Stan nodded to the rattling phone. "You going to get that?"

He puckered his lips, sighed, and slid it across the counter to his son. "You get it. I know it's work, and I want my final twenty-two minutes before I have to go again."

"So why do you want me to answer it?"

"Because you know I'll go in." He grabbed his car keys and wallet and stuffed them in his pants. "See you later."

Chapter Three

Lee struggled to open his eyes. Something covered his mouth. A faint outline of someone stood over him. The bed beneath him rolled forward. The walls flashed by. His head throbbed, his eyes burned. Voices sounded muffled and distant. He tried to speak, but his tongue adhered to the floor of his mouth.

He closed his eyes again.

Darkness.

****

"Freddy, wake up."

Freddy? Who's Freddy? The name didn't register. *But what is my name?* He pushed through the fog. A faint outline of an elderly man leaned over him.

"Freddy, get up you lazy bum."

He opened his eyes and looked at the man standing in front of him. "Who are you?"

The man smiled a toothless grin. "Not as important as who you are."

Fred held his head and tried to sit up. The room appeared surreal, almost glowing. "Am I dead?"

"Not yet, Freddy."

"Why do you keep calling me Freddy?"

The elderly man hopped up on a stool in the corner and spun around like a teenager on a skateboard.

Is this guy for real?

"Well, it's your name, isn't it?"

He didn't know. *Is it*? "I don't remember."

The man reached for the stool like a frog and swung his feet out in front of him. His white robe pushed up to his thighs revealing bony, wrinkled legs. "Well, that's what the nurses called you. Freddy Big Bucks."

Fred sat on the table and smiled. "So, I'm rich. That's encouraging."

The old man swiveled around and let out a squeaky cackle. "Probably true, since most people here are. But if I were you, I don't think I'd be too happy about it." He fanned his right arm out in front of him. "Your being rich may have something to do with *why* you're here."

"Speaking of here…" Fred stood and glanced around the room. Plain eggshell-white walls matched the tile floor. A coral pink curtain hung to his right and two brown doors to his left. "Where is here?"

"You're in Prospect Convalescent Hospital." The man's eyes locked on something behind him. "Almost dead, I reckon."

Fred pivoted around and jumped. A body relaxed inert on the bed. Tubes connected to monitors poured from the male figure's face and arms. "Who is that?"

"Who do you think?"

"That's me?"

The old man laughed and turned on his stool once more. "You're a quick one, ain't cha?"

"But if that's me there…" Fred loosened his collar and moved to a small mirror hanging on the far wall. "Who am I here?" He gasped. The only thing visible was the reflection of the room. "Am I a vampire?"

The crazy coot slapped his knee and howled.

7

Fred wasn't amused.

Wiping his eyes, he joined Fred in the mirror. "You, sir, oh knight-of-the-living-dead, is your mind, imagination, or soul. That has yet to be determined."

Fred stared at the man. His ice-blue eyes seemed to sparkle with wisdom and mischievousness all at once. "Who are you?"

He batted at the air and moved back to his stool. "It's a secret, and I intend to keep it."

"A secret?" Fred cocked his head to one side. "Just tell me who you are."

"Who am I?" The man mocked in a high-pitched voice. "Who are you? What are we, in grade school?" The old man rolled his eyes. "You know, your mind asks way too many questions. Don't you ever accept the answer that is given?"

"What do you mean by that?"

"I guess not." The man kicked up his feet and spun like a child on a merry-go-round at the park.

"Just tell me your name."

"You can call me Bill."

"Bill." Fred sighed and moved to the body on the bed. His hair was matted and his face swollen. A white bandage covered his right eye to the crown of his head. His lips were cracked, and a two-day growth sprouted from the pores in his face. "So, how do I wake myself up?"

"Aw, another question." Bill stopped and peered at the body. "Well, that all depends on whether or not you are his soul."

Fred gazed at the old man with scrunched eyebrows. "I don't understand."

"Why am I not terribly surprised?" Bill rose and

placed his hand on the sleeping man's arm. "If you're a soul, then I'm afraid you'll be meeting your master as soon as…"

Fred gulped. "As soon as what?"

"As soon as you sign off, kick the bucket, croak…" Bill flung his arms out wide to encompass the room. "Move on to the great beyond."

"OK, stop with the metaphors." Fred paced, wringing his hands. "I get it. You're saying I'm dying."

"Sort of. You see, it works like this. You don't really have a choice. Not now, anyway. You had plenty of choices in your life. How you lived your life will determine where you go. If you lived for God, then you'll go up." The old man shot his arm up in the air, and Fred thought it might come out of its socket. "If you didn't, you'll go down." Bill mimed taking off a hat. He brought it to his chest, dropped his chin to his chest, relaxed his shoulders, and began humming *Taps*.

Fred stared at him. "You mean Heaven or Hell?"

Bill pretended to toss his hat and spoke in a high-pitched voice "Paradise, Hades. The great beyond…" He dropped the tone of his voice to a deep baritone. "…the great inferno. The pearly gates, the fires of doom." He began to sing, "Oh sweet chariot—"

"Stop! How do I find out if I'm a soul or not?"

Bill jumped within an inch of Fred's face and ran a hand in front of his eyes. "Do you see spots?"

Fred blinked. "I don't think so."

Bill circled him and brought the back of his hand to Fred's forehead. "How's your body temp? Do you feel cold?"

"No."

"Hmmm." The old man sat back on the stool and

brought his right hand to his chin.

Fred followed him, frantic. "What does that mean?"

The crazy coot eyed him with a gummy smile. "Nothing. I just thought I'd see if your imagination was working."

Fred gritted his teeth. "Not funny, old man."

"Don't be such a stiff. You should lighten up."

"Lighten up? My body is lying on a bed incapacitated. I don't know who I am, or why I'm here, and I'm stuck listening to a mad geezer making jokes." Fred jabbed his finger in the air at the man's face. "Who *are* you?"

The elderly man rounded his shoulders, cleared his throat, and replied with his head held high, "I guess you could call me…" He lifted his arm high in the air and then proceeded to lower it in a dramatic bow as he said in a deep voice, "Your coma companion."

"My what?" Fred rolled his eyes. This guy never quit. "I've never heard of that before."

Bill reached behind the curtain in the middle of the room and brought out a pair of white socks. Sitting like a child, he began to pull one over his bony feet and ankles. "Have you ever been in a coma before?"

"Of course not."

One of his eyebrows lifted, but he kept his focus on the saggy sock. "Have you ever known anyone who's been in a coma before?"

Fred exhaled through his nose. "No."

Bill met his stare and shrugged. "Then why would you have heard of a coma companion? The good news is, the next time you're in a coma, we can skip all this."

Great. Fred shook his head in frustration, or maybe

it was to wake himself up. This had to be a nightmare. *Whoever heard of standing by one's body?* Well outside of horror movies. "What if I'm dreaming, and you're simply a figment of my imagination?"

"Nah," he said, tugging at his robe. "You don't have this good of an imagination." Bill leapt to his feet, then passed his hands over his hips like a model on a runway. "Besides, if it is a dream, could I do this?" Bill grabbed a cup by the side of the bed and tossed it at Fred's shoulder.

"Owe." Not that it really hurt, but he did seem to feel its impact.

"Just thought you should know." The companion shoved his hands through the sides of his hair. It stayed up, making him resemble Einstein.

"Well, I don't want to spend my time in a coma with you. It could be months, and I doubt you're the kind of guy I would normally be seen with." He walked to the door on the left and tried to grab the handle. His hand went through it. "What?"

"Two things you should know. You can't leave because you're stuck to that body. And second, how would you know if you'd hang out with a guy like me or not? You have *amnesia*, remember?" Bill grabbed his gut and shot onto his back, legs kicking in the air.

"I'm glad I can amuse you." Fred walked through the open doorway. It led to a bathroom. "Besides, you said I was rich. Telling by the way you talk, I'm guessing you're a blue-collar kind of guy."

His companion jumped to his feet, dukes out, scowl twisted on his face. "Those are fighting words, mister. Put 'em up."

"I wasn't trying to insult you." He glanced inside

the shower and then back to Bill. "You're kind of ornery to be an angel."

"I ain't no angel. Like I said, the name is Bill." He stuck out his hand. "And I'm not insulted. I just know you're wrong."

"About what?"

When Fred didn't shake his hand, Bill grabbed his own hand and shook it. "Well, Freddy, my son, I'm thinking you are a lonely, lonely guy, who doesn't have any friends."

"What would make you say that?"

Bill rolled his eyes from right to left and then back to Fred. "See any flowers here? Visitors, cards, even a yellow sticky?"

Fred followed his gaze. Other than a box of tissues and a pink pitcher, the counters were bare.

"Trust me. You're alone in this world." Bill jumped in front of him and smiled from ear to ear. "Well, except for me, you lucky guy."

Chapter Four

The door opened, and a nurse entered with a tray. She walked past Fred and set it on the table next to the bed. She lifted and examined the body's right wrist. "Hello, Mr. Avarice. I'm Kari. How are you feeling today?"

Fred moved next to her. "Are you talking to me?"

Kari didn't face him but continued to talk to the body. "Don't feel like talking, huh?" A small smile played on her pretty features. "Well, can't say I blame you. You've been here for almost a month and not one person has visited you."

She raised his head and readjusted his pillow. "I know I can't prove it, but I believe human contact aids in recovering from these sorts of things. The doctors say you're healthy. Can't figure out why you're still sleeping."

Fred glanced at Bill. "She can't see me?"

"Sure she can. You're the stiff she's talking to."

"You mean the body."

"Formality. But yes."

He felt like a ghost. Maybe if he got closer. He pushed next to her and ran a hand over her eyes. She didn't flinch. Just kept tending to the job at hand.

She lifted a clear bag from the metal stand to the left of the headboard, detached it, and tossed it in the red bucket to her left. "You know, you remind me of my older brother. I wish you could meet him. He's a major in the Army infantry. He left for Iraq about the time you came to join us here." She grabbed a new IV bag, placed it on the metal stand, and attached it to the tube that went into his arm. "Guess in some ways, you're like him in spirit." She grabbed a pan from under a shelf and walked to the bathroom.

Fred turned to Bill, who watched from the corner. "A month? How's that possible? It's only been a few hours."

"Time for us is irrelevant. We don't move in the same reality."

"So, this *is* my imagination."

"I didn't say that."

The nurse entered again with a pan full of water and a washcloth. She sat in the chair next to the body with a dampened cloth and wiped his face.

Fred looked at her name badge. Kari Jensen.

"I wonder who you were, Mr. Avarice. You must be well-off or you wouldn't be here." She wiped his neck. "Most nurses hate this part of the job, but for me, it's like being a part of a wonderful ministry." She flipped the cloth over. "It's the orderly's job to clean you, but I enjoy it. I like attending to someone who can't take care of himself." She pulled his gown down to his waist and brought the washcloth to his chest. "So, what did you do wrong, Mr. Avarice? The other nurses call you Freddy Big Bucks. But I like you. So, I'll take good care of you. Deal?" She finished his bath, poured the dirty water into the bathroom sink, and then moved to go. "Thanks for talking with me. You've been a dear. I'll see you on Thursday."

The door swung shut and the room was once again

quiet.

Fred walked to the chair next to the bed. The body looked unfamiliar, and yet it was him, wasn't it? "She called me, Mr. Avarice."

"I suppose that's your name." Bill perched on his stool the way a toad sits on a rock.

Fred sighed. "So, how do I figure out if I'm just dwelling in some crazy dream, or if I'm a soul who is ready to take the ultimate journey?"

"You don't."

The haze of the room felt dreamlike, and yet everything seemed real. Fred rested his elbows on the edge of the mattress and exhaled. *Why am I here*? He didn't even remember who *he* was. Frustration seethed through his mind. He faced Bill. "If you're my companion, then shouldn't you entertain me? I could use the distraction."

"Is that what you want me to do?" Bill laughed. "Entertain you?"

"I don't know what I want. I just can't figure out why you'd want to hang out with a guy in a coma. Who are you?"

The old man placed his hand to his chest. "*Moi*?"

"Yes, where do you come from? If you're not an angel, what's your purpose here?"

He sat up straight. "To be your companion and..." He pointed to the far corner the room. "Oh no, Freddy. It can't be. I see a light."

"A light?" He squinted. "Where? What does that mean?"

"A bright one means you were good, and a dark one means something else. Bad, very bad."

"What's bad?"

Bill cleared his throat. "That you'll be going down under, and I don't mean a trip to Australia."

Fred stared at the corner. With the exception of a few dust bunnies, it appeared empty. "I don't see anything." He glanced back at Bill. "There's nothing there. Now stop trying to change the subject and finish telling me why you're here."

Bill stood next to him. "I'm here to help you remember."

"Remember what? Who I was? You can do that?"

He shook his head and stepped to the mirror. "To help you remember when you said *yes* to decadence. The path your life is on is a road that leads to eternal *da da doom.*"

He stared at Bill, stunned. The goofy little guy now seemed wise and controlled. Were his antics some sort of test? He laughed.

"Got a joke to share, Freddy?" Bill asked.

"At least call me Fred, okay?"

"Okay, Frrreeeddd." Bill grinned. "You ever read *Moby Dick?*"

"I don't remember."

"Of course." Bill patted Fred's back and turned to face him. "Well, Captain Ahab was obsessed with finding Moby Dick, the great white whale that took his leg. Reason told Ahab it was a fool's journey, and he would die trying. But his desire to find his prize was too great for good sense to break through." Bill narrowed his eyes and poked Fred several times in the torso. "I'm afraid that's you, Mr. Avarice. You are Captain Ahab."

"Ouch! Stop that." He stepped back, rubbing his chest. "You don't even know me."

"I know your kind. I've been watching rich dupes

like you for decades. You come in here wealthy enough to stay until you die. It's sad. The whole lot of you…too busy building financial empires to take stock of your lives."

"Look, I don't even remember what got me here, so, you can hardly judge me." He paced, scratching his head. "All I care about is what I can do to change it. Do you know that?"

"I do."

He walked up behind Bill and looked in the mirror. "How?"

"Stand here." Bill pointed to the tile in front of the mirror and stepped to the side. "Now, look hard into the glass."

Fred walked forward, his reflection still non-existent. *I'm a vampire.* "This is dumb. We've already established I can't see myself. I'm not there." He turned away, hands on hips. "Neither are you."

Bill chuckled. "Of course not. As we discussed, you're merely a phantom or a soul. Those things don't have reflections. Now look again, and no matter what happens, don't blink." Bill placed his hands on Fred's shoulders and pointed him back to the mirror. "Think of this as a portal, a doorway to the past."

"What *will* happen?"

Bill grinned. "You'll remember."

Chapter Five

Sitting on a yellow embroidered bedspread, Fred glanced down at his hands and turned them over. They were tiny.

Where am I?

A soft, amber light glowed in the room. Green curtains with yellow flowers decorated the windows on his right. He turned to his left. Mommy? *She sat next to him on the bed. Her cheeks soaked with tears. "Please, Tom, don't leave. I thought you loved me. Please!"*

Fred's father didn't seem to hear her. Instead, he continued throwing his clothes from dresser drawers into a duffel bag on the end of the bed.

"We can work this out. It's not too late," she said. "I'll forgive you for everything."

Movement to his right made the man turn around. An Indian woman with long black hair stood in the doorway with a bushel of keys tight in her hand.

His dad looked at the woman, and a funny smile flashed across her dark features.

His mom peered her way, too.

The woman's smile disappeared. Her face turned red, and she left the room.

His dad tossed the bag's strap over his shoulder and crossed to the door.

Fred scooted off the mattress at the foot of the bed. "Daddy?"

His dad turned back, lifted his hand to his son's shoulder, patted it a few times, and continued out the door.

He didn't even say good-bye. *He looked back at his mom. She was crying* so *loud. "Tom, come back!" Her body shook.*

The front screen door slammed. She jumped up and almost knocked Freddy over. She rushed into the living room and out the door.

He followed and grabbed onto her leg. His daddy's truck squealed out of the driveway.

She screamed.

Within seconds, the taillights disappeared in the distance.

Freddy took her tear-soaked hands in his chubby fingers. "Mommy, why did daddy leave?"

"Daddy's gone," was all she said. Then she grabbed him, lifted him on her hip, and hugged him tight.

He gasped, unable to breathe.

Her grip lessened as she wiped her eyes, and he managed to wriggle free. She let go, then shuffled back to the bedroom, and slumped to the floor.

He followed and knelt beside her. Unable to fully grasp the emotion he felt. He just wanted his mom to feel better. It hurt to see her so sad. "Everything will be okay, Mommy."

That seemed to make her cry more. She buried her head in the brown shag carpet and squealed, then pushed against the ground like a dog with a bone and cried so hard the floor vibrated. "We have no money! You've left us with nothing."

Fred backed away, his heart pounding. "Mommy,

Mommy…please stop!" You're scaring me.

She calmed down but didn't lift her head.

"Mommy, I'm here." He walked to her side, laid his hand against her head, and stroked her hair. It was soft.

She looked up, and he barely recognized her. Her face was swollen and red. Yellow goop ran from her nose, and black ink poured from her eyes. When she wiped it with the back of her arm, it smeared across her cheeks. She crawled up onto the bed and pulled him into her lap. "I love you, Freddy." She threw the bedspread over his legs and closed her eyes.

They lay like that all night. Daddy never returned.

****

Fred's eyes shot open. He gazed at the body across the room. It looked worn and sweaty. "What happened?" He leaned against the wall and glanced back at the mirror. "How did I go back there?"

Bill peered up from the floor where he sat playing solitaire. "You went somewhere, did you?"

"Yeah, I remember. It was my earliest memory, just two days before my fourth birthday. The day my father left."

He went back to his game. "Significant then?"

"Yes, but for what reason?

"Oh crumb biscuit!" Bill smacked the top of the deck. "I should have played that card earlier. Now I'm going to lose." He peered over at Fred. "You need to find that out yourself, Big Bucks. There are no hidden reasons for why we are the way we are." He tossed another card from his hand to the floor. "Like these cards, each one played alters our next action. Obviously, your father leaving affected you later on.

20

How? I don't know. Only you can discover that."

"I don't know if I want to."

Bill's expression turned somber. "Freddy, your time may be short. You don't want to face the dark light without evaluating your soul."

"I suppose, if it's real."

"You don't want to find out after the fact. Trust me."

Fred stared back at the mirror. Sparks shot in the glass, and the silver reflection turned to a pool of mercury, and then everything blurred. His destination unknown.

****

Stan brought two bottles of water into the den and handed one to Melissa. The lights were low, and the fireplace raged like his heart. A soft glow made the room appear amber and peaceful.

"Thank you." She pushed a strand of red hair over her ear and maneuvered to face him on the leather sofa. "So, are you sure you have to work tonight? Because I hear the original *Superman* movie will be on TV."

He touched her hand and smiled. "I doubt you want me to stay home to watch an old movie."

She inched closer to him and kissed his nose. "Well, that was my alibi, this is my motive." She touched her lips to his.

His heart accelerated. They'd been dating for almost a year, and he knew it was time to make the ultimate commitment and marry her. But that thought was a cold shower to his mind. He pulled back and stared into her hazel eyes. She was beautiful, smart, accepted his lifestyle. *What am I waiting for?*

"You've got that look again. What is it?"

"Are you content with our relationship?"

She nibbled on the side of her lip, a sign he knew to be dangerous. The answer already given.

No. He frowned. "So, I guess you're not."

"Well, I'd like to know we have other plans in the works. Even if we can't make them come true right now." She fingered a crease in his shirt. "I know it would make your dad happy."

Did he love her enough to marry her, or was this about his father? Stan always assumed he'd know the right girl when he met her. Like skywriting to his heart. But then, in his line of work, he didn't have a lot of time for intimacy. Maybe their connection was palpable, but he was blind.

"Penny for your thoughts?"

He pinched his lips in a half-grin. "Sorry, just weighing the future, I guess. It's not easy being a cop's wife, you know?"

"It's not easy being anybody's wife, I'm sure." She ran a hand down his arm. "I think if the love is there, the rest will work itself out."

Love. There it was. His dilemma. *Do I love her? Is it enough?* Growing up, Stan watched his mom and dad with awed fascination. Never had he seen such devotion between two human beings and yet, they fought often for one reason—George's insatiable urge to place himself in harm's way. A cop's mantra. Stan hated the irony. All her worrying about her husband and she died first.

The radio squawked from the counter in the kitchen. "All available police officers, code thirty, please advise."

His heart leapt. Stan jumped off the couch and

picked it up. "Heller. Go ahead."

"Two-forty-three possible ten-fifty-four delta. Officer down at Burlington Avenue. Over."

Angst and urgency shot adrenaline through his body. He sighed and brought the mike to his mouth. "Denver Thirty-two. Go ahead."

"What's your ten-twenty?"

"Ten minutes out."

"Respond to four-eighty-seven Burlington Avenue. Proceed with caution. Suspect may be armed. Over."

"Ten-four." He placed the radio back on the counter and grabbed his holster and strapped it on.

Melissa walked next to him and touched his shoulder. "Is everything okay?"

"I've got to go. An officer has been shot." He kissed her cheek, grabbed his jacket, and practically flew out the door.

Within minutes, the suburbs turned into lush trees, tall-gated walls, and long circular driveways. His destination lay at the end of the block.

He pulled around the roadblock, through an iron gate, and parked at the back of the mansion. The parking lot was filled with cops and paramedics scrambling in all directions. Sirens and squawking radios filled the air. He grabbed his notepad from the dashboard and tucked it in his coat jacket. The captain knocked on his window before he could open the door. Stan rolled it down. "Hey, Cap. Crazy mess, huh? What's the verdict?"

"We have enough cops here. Turn around and go to the station." The man's expression was stern. "There are some things that need your immediate attention."

"Don't be absurd. I'm here now…" He pulled the

car handle.

The captain nudged the door back. "Detective Heller, don't argue with me, return to the station. We'll discuss it back at the office."

Stan opened his mouth to object.

"You value your job, you'll follow this order." The captain turned around and whispered in a fellow officer's ear. The cop nodded and motioned for Stan to pull around.

What's going on? He shook his head and started the engine. Sometimes the captain could be such a jerk. He drove past an emergency vehicle and out the gate, keeping an eye on his rear-view mirror. It was obvious with all the chaos; they could use an extra hand. Sending him away was bizarre.

The traffic to the precinct was heavier than usual, but he didn't mind. It gave him time to chew over what might have caused his boss to act so strange. *I must know the victim.* They said two-forty-three. That meant a cop had been attacked. It could be a colleague of his. *But who?* Suddenly, fear gripped his throat. *No!* He did an illegal U-turn in the middle of an intersection. Several cars honked, one just missed his right bumper.

The traffic on the way back was far from comforting. If he'd had an army tank, he'd have driven over each and every car. At the mansion gate, he glimpsed the sight of a black body bag being loaded into the rear of an ambulance. His heart raced. Panic, anger, fear, sadness—all at once a dozen emotions scoured his system. He pulled his car over to the curb and walked up the driveway onto the property. It didn't take but a second for the captain to spot him. The cop's eyes revealed all he needed to know. It wasn't irritation that had caused his boss to be a jerk, but dread about revealing the truth.

Chapter Six

"Wake up, Freddy," his mom said from somewhere in the distance. "Come on, honey, we have to get going."

Fred blinked a few times and saw he was in his childhood bed. His mom stood beside him, dressed in a green grocery store uniform, pinning her hair.

"Mom?"

"Oh, good, you're awake. Come on, sweetheart. You've got to get dressed. We're moving."

"Again?" He rubbed his eyes and sat up. His toys and clothes were already packed in boxes and brown paper bags, waiting by the door. "But why? We like it here."

His mom cupped her palm under his chin. "We don't have enough money to stay here anymore, and once again, your father's child support check didn't arrive. We need to find cheaper housing."

"But what about our neighbor, Rosa? We can't just leave her behind." He pushed his lower lip into a pout. It rarely worked, but it was always worth a shot. "And what about school?"

"Honey, we can always come and visit Rosa. And I'll call the school and let them know you'll be out today." She kissed his nose and stood. "Now get dressed. I have to work this evening, and we need to find a place first."

Fred swung his legs over the side of the bed and got to his feet. The wooden floor felt icy, and he sat back down, arms crossed in defiance. His mom kept the heater off to save money on gas. "It's too cold."

"Here." *She reached into one of the paper bags and pulled out a rolled pair of tube socks.* "Put these on." *She tossed them on the bed next to him and left with a box in her arms.*

He put on the socks, then shuffled to the bathroom, and turned on the faucet. After waiting a minute for the water to warm, he gave up and placed a washcloth under the water. Another cold bath and probably dry toast for breakfast.

He scowled at his reflection in the mirror. Something flickered in the mirror. What was that? *He flipped around. There was nothing but a shower stall.* That's funny. I thought I saw a man. *He looked back at the mirror. His freckled face stared back at him. He shrugged and reached for his toothbrush. Forgoing an icy shower, he just brushed his teeth and combed his hair.*

"Son, are you ready?" *His mom yelled from the dining area.* "The landlord will be here any moment, and we need to be long gone."

Fred glanced around his small bedroom and sighed. His five-foot one frame could almost lie wall to wall. He hoped their next place would be bigger, but he doubted it. He grabbed his backpack, and the box of toys on his dresser, and then plodded into the living room.

His mother waited, foot tapping, keys in hand. "Boy, you sure are pokey today." *She tousled his hair and motioned for him to follow.* "Let's go."

The two walked out to the curb where a brown Pinto awaited them. She unlocked the trunk, and he set his stuff in the open space. Across the street, he noticed a teenage boy collecting money from their neighbors for mowing his lawn. "I can't wait to be a teenager," Fred said.

"Why do you want to grow up so fast?" She slammed the trunk closed and let him in the passenger side. "I like you just the way you are. I've been thinking about not feeding you. Then maybe you'll stop growing."

Ignoring her poor attempt at a joke, he climbed inside and waited for her to join him before answering. "Because then I can help you pay the bills, and we won't have to ever move again."

She caressed his face with the back of her hand. "Oh, Freddy, I'm so sorry things have been rough. Once I finish my night classes, maybe I can get work at a good paying job, huh?"

He smiled. "Yes, Mom."

She kissed the top of his head, started the engine, and they were off.

****

"There's one!" Fred pointed to a three-story, olive-green building with a "Now Renting" sign posted on the lawn in front.

His mom swung over to the curb and parked. "Worth a shot. Come on."

They both got out and climbed the stairs to the office. Inside, a lady sat at her desk writing on huge sheets of paper, separated by carbon. She looked up and smiled. "Welcome to Buena Vista. May I help you?"

At least, she was friendlier than the last ten places they'd been to. "Yes, we were interested in finding an apartment." His mom motioned over her shoulder. "We saw your sign out front."

"We have a studio left. Would you like to see it?"

Fred didn't miss his mother's disappointed frown. "What's a studio?" he asked.

"A one-room apartment." His mom glanced at her watch. "We'd like to see it."

"Sure thing. Let me just grab a key." The woman walked to a cabinet on the wall. She opened the door and sorted through a bunch of metal rings. "Here we are." She withdrew one and then waved for them to follow her. "It's on the top floor, which is always nice when you're trying to sleep." They walked up a flight of stairs, and she reached to unlock the knob. "Always hated the thought of people walking on my head." She smiled, pushed open the door, and motioned for them to enter. "It's pretty roomy for a studio. Hope you like it."

Fred's mom nudged him forward, and they stepped inside. The carpet was brown and the walls white, but she was right, it was big. "We'll take it," his mom said.

"Wonderful. Let's just go draw up the papers."

As they walked back to the office, Fred peered around the courtyard. There were fruit trees, birds of paradise, park benches, Tiki posts, and a swimming pool. He was glad they were going to live here. It was how he imagined Hawaii. When he made it back to the office, his mom was already seated.

"Here. Sign this form." The woman handed his mom a yellow paper on a clipboard and turned around to dig in a small bin. "I'll just need a five-hundred-dollar deposit and the first month's rent."

His mom stopped the pen and stared at her with an opened mouth. "That's a lot."

She turned back and smiled. "How would you like to pay for that?"

"I...um...I can pay the five hundred deposit, but I'm a little short for the other five hundred right now." Fred had seen the same look a dozen times already that day. Her eyes welled with tears and her mouth quivered.

"I'm sorry, but it's our policy." The woman folded her hands on the desk and sat forward. "We've had too many people skip out, so we can't make any exceptions."

"Thanks anyway." His mom handed the clipboard back, draped her right arm around Fred's shoulders, and escorted him out the door.

"But I liked that place," he said as they scurried down the steps.

"It's too much. We couldn't have afforded the five hundred a month anyway." She looked at her watch again. "We'll keep looking."

For another three hours, they drove from complex to complex searching for a place to stay. By dusk, the paper was covered in red X's. Most of the apartments were already rented, some were what his mother called "roach infested," and others were too expensive for their budget.

"Mommy, what'll we do if we don't find a home?"

She gave him a partial grin. Her eyes were red and tired. "I wish I knew."

Chapter Seven

"Ready. Fire!" The air reverberated with the crack of seven rifles firing at once. "Ready. Fire!"

Stan jolted at the pop of the guns.

"Ready. Fire!"

His eyes blinked erratically. He shuddered.

Taps began to play as a line of officers dressed in blue uniforms, complete with gloves and shined shoes, draped a flag over his father's coffin. The man in the box had been two years away from getting his gold watch; instead, he'd finish his term sealed in the ground.

"Would you like to say anything?" Pastor Ron asked.

Stan nodded and stepped forward. His voice rasped as he began, "My father was an amazing officer. He dedicated his life to the force and to keeping this city safe." A tear escaped to run down Stan's cheek. He batted it away and continued, "For those who knew him, they would understand this is how he would want to go. In the line of duty, and now home with his wife." His voice cracked and he couldn't hold back the pain any longer. "I'll miss him." He tossed a white rose on the flag-covered coffin and stepped back.

The pastor walked to a small podium and said, "Let us pray."

The crowd bowed their heads.

"We pray today to commit the spirit of George Wayne Heller into your hands. We know that someday we shall see him again. Give peace to the family and to his friends with full assurance he is now with you. Amen."

The crowd echoed his amen.

"Thank you all for coming."

The mourners filed past Stan one by one, offering their condolences and shaking his hand. He couldn't hear their words or recognize their faces. The world blurred into a sea of watercolors.

Melissa looped her arm through his. "Let me get you home."

He nodded and walked with her to the car. His mind numb, he didn't talk during the short ride to his house. A weight he couldn't fathom rested heavy on his chest, suffocating him. The *if only thoughts* sounding in his head. *If only* his father hadn't taken that second shift. *If only* he'd married someone sooner so his dad could see his grandchildren. *If only*—

"Are you going to be okay?" Melissa laid a hand on his knee. Until now, he hadn't realized they were parked in front of his house.

"I'll be fine."

She touched the back of his hand. "You want me to come in? I could make you dinner."

He shook his head, not meeting her gaze. "I'm not really hungry."

"I'll check on you later, okay?"

He nodded, opened and closed the car door, trudged up the steps, and placed a key in the knob. Every motion reminded him of his father. He shoved the door open and exhaled. The empty house burned his senses. Shadows from the afternoon sun fell over the entryway adding to his gloom. It was his father's home, and its owner was gone.

Chapter Eight

Fred blinked at the mirror in front of him. Somehow he had returned to the hospital room.

Bill hovered inches behind him, staring over his shoulder into the glass. "That's quite the childhood you've had. Almost caused an old man to get misty." He pretended to wipe under his eye, then flicked his fingers into the air.

Fred swatted at the air. "You saw my childhood?"

"Only what you described out loud. You talk in your sleep."

"Funny." Fred walked back to his body and sat on the edge of the bed. "I don't like seeing that. It's depressing."

"What happened to your mom? Did you ever find a place to stay?"

"No, not really." Fred sighed and stared at the tubes running from his body's arms and face.

The elderly man sat on the floor, pulled his legs up to his chest, and wrapped his robe over his knees. "No? So, you're starting to remember?"

"Some."

"Where did you live?"

Emotion Fred hadn't felt in years swelled in his throat. It hurt to speak. "We slept in the car for two days, before I went to live with my aunt."

****

Stan looked through the peephole at the pretty blonde and sighed. *This will not end well.* He unlocked the deadbolt and opened the door. "Hi."

Melissa glanced up. "Can we talk?"

He swallowed. Since the funeral a few weeks ago, he had successfully avoided her. But it was time. They needed to have it out. "Sure." He stepped back and allowed her to enter.

Like any other visit, she walked to the study and removed her coat.

"Would you like anything to drink? I have a few diet sodas left."

"No, I'm good." She perched on the arm of the couch, obviously ready for battle.

With his head hung low, Stan sat across from her. He felt like a child in trouble. Maybe he could soften the blow. "I'm sorry I haven't returned your calls. I just haven't felt like talking."

Her hand touched his chin, forcing his eyes to meet hers and he saw her pain. "Yes, that's what I wanted to talk to you about. It doesn't make sense that you'd push me away. I thought you loved me."

"This isn't about you, Melissa. This is about me handling my father's death."

She dropped her hand in her lap and stared at it. "No, I'm talking about you not trusting me enough. How could we ever marry if—"

He raised an eyebrow. "Who said anything about marriage?"

Her stare shot to his. "You mean you don't want to?"

Get out the shovel and start digging. "I don't know. Things are a bit out of sorts right now, Melissa.

35

How can you be this selfish?"

"Selfish?" She jumped to her feet. "Are you kidding me? I'm here because I want you to let me in. To let me help you. And you're pushing me out of your life."

"Maybe I don't want help. Maybe I need to process this in my own way." *Maybe I don't want you in my life.* He sighed. Any energy he had to fight was buried with his father. "Look, just give me time. Back off a bit. This isn't about you."

Fire flared in her eyes. "Back off? You obviously don't need me, so I'll make this simple. We're through."

"Melissa." He reached for her hand, but she flung it off.

"I want a man in my life who wants me with him in the good times and bad. You're obviously not *that* man." She wrapped her coat around her shoulders and stormed out.

His vision glazed over. He knew he should be sad or upset, but his emotions remained numb. He grabbed his keys from the coffee table. He just needed to keep busy with work. It was the only time he felt remotely sane.

Chapter Nine

Stan walked down a narrow, vacant hospital hallway. The fluorescent light at the end of the corridor flickered and buzzed in complaint. He stared at the numbers above the doors. Seventy-four, five, six… His loafers squeaked on the waxed floor, and he secretly hoped he didn't wake any residents.

Seventy-seven. *This is it*. He glanced at his notepad of paper. According to his dad's notes, the suspect shot Avarice in the head at close range. The crime scene only held two sets of fingerprints—Avarice and that of a dead man. The secretary's statement said that one of the owners, Asher Melton, was the last person scheduled to meet with him. She described him as a burly man, possibly in his early fifties with a beard and brown crew cut. But they had not been able to find him.

For over a month, Stan had searched for leads in the case that could aid in finding his father's killer, and so far, all of Stan's leads were dead. *Literally*. When he heard that the first victim, Lee Avarice still lived, he almost kissed the office clerk who told him. He needed Lee's statement and couldn't wait to get it. Glancing away from his book, he reached for the doorknob.

"Excuse me." A nurse walked toward him. "Can I help you?"

Stan pulled a badge out of his inside jacket pocket and held it up. "I'm Detective Stan Heller. I need to speak with Lee Avarice regarding a case."

She shook her head. "Lee? You must have the wrong room. This patient's name is Fredrick."

He didn't have time to explain details to some nurse. Time was short, and this patient was one of the few witnesses left in a long line of murders. "Yes, Fredrick *Lee* Avarice. After he left home, he began using his middle name." He produced a smile. "Look, Ms.?" He glanced at her name badge. "Jensen. I really need to interview Mr. Avarice. He's the only witness we have in a very important investigation."

"I'm sorry, but you won't be able to interview him."

Deep breath. He squared his shoulders, ready for battle. "Look, we've lost over a dozen businessmen and one cop in the last two months. He was the first man shot and the only one to survive. If I need to get a warrant, then I will."

Her perfect pink lips curved into a smile. "Detective, I wasn't trying to play hardball. I meant he's in a coma. You can go in, but I don't think you'll get much information out of him."

All hope fell at his feet. "Oh, I see." *Now what?* "Thank you, Ms. Jensen. I think I'll still go in." Pushing the door open, he stepped inside. The gentle hum of equipment and a soft glow from the light by the headboard offered the still ambiance in the room. From Lee's chart, Stan learned he was six-foot-one, a slender two hundred pounds, and by the giggles he'd heard at the entrance of the hospital, apparently eye candy for the ladies. He wondered if the last detail was enough for the man's wife to serve him divorce papers.

Stan sensed something behind him and turned back

to the door.

Nurse Jensen grinned.

"Since you're sticking around," Stan said, "I have a question for you, too."

"Yes, Detective?"

"Does the hospital keep records of anybody who has visited him in the last month?"

"That's simple." She stepped forward. "No one has."

"Really?" Stan lifted his right eyebrow. "He's still legally married for a few more months. Not even his wife showed?"

She frowned. "No, I'm afraid not."

"Do you know if she was ever contacted?"

"As far as I know."

"That's interesting." Stan bit the end of his pen and scanned his notes again. Reports said Lee rented an apartment only a night before the incident. His wife insisted he move out, but during her interview with Stan's father, she seemed heartbroken. Maybe she wasn't the grieving widow after all. "So, what's the chance he'll wake up?"

Her forlorn expression spoke volumes. She clasped her hands in front of her and sighed. "We are a special care facility, Detective, not a regular hospital. Most people don't come here unless the medical community has lost all hope for their recovery. Mr. Avarice is healthy overall, but his brain shows little activity. There is a slight chance he could wake up, but the more likely scenario is he'll be in this state for the rest of his life. However short that might be." Her eyes went wide and she covered her mouth. "Oh no! Look, I'm not a doctor, and I shouldn't have said all that. I assume you'll be putting it in your report?"

He sensed her worry and offered a reassuring grin. "Look, if I need it for any reason, I'll consult with his doctor. Deal?"

She visibly exhaled and smiled. "Thank you."

"No, thank you." He returned her smile. She was pretty in a natural sort of way. Not all made up like most the girls he knew. Her auburn hair was pulled up on the sides, fastened by a large silver clip. Her large, almond-shaped chocolate eyes danced like someone high on life. She wore a loose white dress, that didn't compliment her thin curves, and her pale complexion indicated she probably didn't get out much. As she covered her bright smile, he noticed chewed nails—an indication of anxiety. Using his detective skills, he deduced this woman was likely a recluse who liked working in a facility where social skills weren't part of the package.

He cleared his throat. "Well, Ms. Jensen, if you don't mind, I'm going to sit here a while and think."

She stared at him for a moment, before a shadow of understanding appeared on her face. "Oh, of course." She smirked and left him alone with the sleeping man.

The door swung closed, just as his cell phone rang in his pocket. He pulled it out and glanced at the screen. *Melissa.* He couldn't deal with her right now. The fact she broke up with him just because he asked her to back off was proof she wasn't the *one*. *Why couldn't she understand?* His father's killer and his own grief took first priority. He sighed and stuffed the phone back in his pocket. They were better off going their separate ways.

Stan stared at the docile man. The shallow breaths

that moved his chest cavity in a recurrent motion remained his only sign of life. "Right now, you're all I've got, Mr. Avarice. Please don't let me down."

****

After driving south for two hours, Fred and his mother climbed the stairs of a townhouse just outside the city and knocked on a blue door. A moment later it opened, revealing his Auntie Tori. Purple velour sweats hugged her thin frame, and a pair of chopsticks held her brunette hair high on her head.

"Hi, sis," his mom said.

"Rebecca!" She stepped around the screen door and embraced her neck. "Oh, it is so good to see you. I didn't know you were coming down. I would have changed."

"Sorry, it wasn't planned. I didn't know where else to go." His mom pulled back and grinned through her tears. "Can we come in?"

"Of course." Tori held open the screen for them to enter.

They stepped inside the entryway. The family pictures scattered along the walls were crooked, almost as if on purpose. Books lined several shelves and a portrait of his mother as a child rested on the fireplace mantle. Sheer brown curtains hung to the floor, and the smell of bacon grease wafted through the air.

"Have a seat," his aunt said, pointing to a flowered couch. "Can I get you anything to drink?"

"I'd like some Kool-Aid," Fred said.

She laughed. "I'm afraid I don't have any Kool-Aid, but how about some juice? I think I have apple."

He nodded.

"Rebecca?"

His mom flicked her hand in the air. "No, I'm fine."

Tori turned for the kitchen, and Fred sat down on the cream-colored shag carpet. A small gray kitten walked next to him and grazed his body with her own. Fred ran his hand along her back, and she rose in response. Once past him, the kitten yawned, stuck out her paws, and stretched.

His aunt returned with an amber-filled glass and handed it to him.

He took the cup. "What's your cat's name?"

"What do you say, Freddy?" his mom asked.

He glanced at her, and then back to his aunt. "Thank you."

"You're welcome." She smiled. "And her name's Marshmallow."

Fred furrowed his brow. "But she's gray."

"It's a long story." She sat in the rocking chair and looked at her sister. "So, what brings the two of you to San Diego?"

His mom bit her lip and took a deep breath. "I lost my job and our place. We've been living in our car."

"Oh, honey." Tori sat next to her sister on the couch. "Why didn't you come to me sooner? You can stay here as long as you like."

His mom shook her head and wiped at the tears trickling down her cheeks. "Thanks, but I need to ask you something bigger."

Tori grabbed a tissue from the end table by the couch and passed it to her. "Sure, what is it?"

"I found a solution to help us get situated, but it will take me away for six months." His mom glanced over at him. "I enlisted in the Army this morning and

need you to watch Freddy while I'm in training."

"What?" Fred's heart fluttered. "Mom, you can't leave me!"

Tori peered at Fred with her mouth open. "I...um...I've never taken care of a kid before. I wouldn't know what to do."

"Mom, you can't leave me," he said again, sitting forward on his knees.

"Tori, I've seen you. You were always great with the kids around us growing up. It will only be for six months. Not forever." She scooted to the edge of the couch and snatched another tissue. "I know it is a big inconvenience, but you know me, Tori. You know I wouldn't ask you if I had any other option."

"I know. But what about his father?"

His mom peeked at him, slow in picking her words. "He's been out of the picture for a while. He's lost the right." She stood and dabbed at her eyes. "I'm supposed to report at the processing station in a few hours, so I need to go. Can you do this for me?"

His aunt rose from the couch, her eyes wide and mouth still open. "Wow! That soon? I don't know."

"Please, Tori."

She let out a long sigh as she stared at him. "Okay. But just six months."

Fred ran to his mom and grabbed her waist. This wasn't happening. He'd heard wrong. She couldn't leave him, right? Didn't she love him? First dad and now her? "You can't go, Mom." His voice hoarse, choked with emotion.

She tipped his chin up and said, "Walk me out?" Then she looked back at her sister. "I'm sorry about this. I owe you big time." She reached over and *squeezed her tight. "I love you."*

"I love you, too, sis. You go do what you need to do. We'll be waiting for you when you get back."

"Thank you." His mom took Fred by the hand and they walked to the car. She unlocked the trunk and placed his suitcase and an overnight bag on the curb at his side.

"Mom, don't go. Please."

She squatted and met his eyes. "Sweetie, I would love nothing more than to stay here with you. But we both know I don't have enough money to do that right now."

"But your classes. You were going to teach school."

She sighed. "I had to quit. The tuition was too much." She squeezed his hand. "But this is better. You'll live with your aunt for just a little while, and I'll be home in time for your eleventh birthday. Won't that be good?"

He nodded and tried to smile.

"Then I'll qualify for on-post housing, and you can come join me, okay?"

"I love you, Mom."

Crying, she reached out and pulled him into her arms. They hugged each other tight. He could still smell a hint of rose in her hair from the sponge bath that morning. Her face was soft against his cheek, and her arms tight around his torso.

Her breath warmed his ear as she whispered, "I love you very, very much. And don't you ever think this has anything to do with my love for you. You understand?"

He nodded against her shoulder. Snot threatened

to pour out, but he sniffed it back in. "I'll miss you so much."

She kissed the top of his head and set his feet back on the sidewalk. He didn't let go of her neck, so she tickled his armpits. Despite how sad he felt, he giggled.

She stood up and straightened her dress. "Now, you be a good boy for your aunt. I better not get any reports otherwise. Okay?"

"Okay."

His aunt stepped to the curb and took Fred's hand. His mom waved one last time, climbed in her Pinto, pulled out into traffic, and was lost in a sea of cars.

****

Fred blinked. He wiped at his moist eyes. *I hate this.* Movement sounded behind him. He turned. He was back in his room, and Bill was having fun with a man in a suit sitting by his bed. "What are you doing?"

Bill punched, poked, and slapped at the man. Like a hologram, his arms went right through him. "It's fun. You should try it." He leaned back and jump-kicked him in the face.

"No, thanks."

Bill stopped and placed a hand on his hip. "So, how was your last trip?"

"What, I didn't murmur to you this time?"

"Yeah, but I want to hear how it affected you."

"Maybe later." Fred wiped a hand over his face and walked next to the stranger in his room. "Who's this guy anyway?"

Bill stuck his finger in his own mouth and then placed it in the inert man's ear.

"Stop that."

The crazy man smiled. "I suppose he is a detective

of some sort. Seems real interested in talking to you about what, or should I say *who*, put you here."

"A detective?" Fred rubbed his hands together and faced the man. "I wish I could wake up and tell him my story."

The old man stopped messing with the man and faced Fred with a curious grin. "What *is* your story?"

Fred started to open his mouth and then pursed his lips together. *Good question.* "Well, I guess I don't quite remember all that yet. But if I woke up, I'd probably remember."

Bill pointed at the mirror. "You need more time inside."

He shook his head and turned to face the window. "I don't like what I see when I'm in there. Too many bad memories. I think I'd rather not."

A penny flew just millimeters by Fred's ear, landing on the windowsill.

"Ouch!"

"It didn't even touch you."

He frowned. "Well, it could have."

Bill rolled his eyes. "Still not getting this whole spirit versus reality thing, are you?"

"So why'd you throw it at me?"

"Because you said you didn't want to remember."

"So?"

"So?" Bill's eyes bulged. "You can't change anything if you don't know where you went wrong."

Fred glanced back at the mirror. It didn't have any sides or a frame, in fact, it looked like any ordinary mirror. And yet, its power was that of any time machine. The reflection seemed to be a portal to his soul. He stared hard at the glass surface, almost afraid of what would happen next. "Do I really want to change?"

Bill lay on top of Fred's body and mimed the coma man's pose. "You have to ask?"

"Fine, I'll go." He turned back unsure, once again afraid of the past.

Chapter Ten

"*Sam!*" *Fred yelled to his best friend across the courtyard.*

The redheaded boy glanced up and smiled. "Hey, you ready?"

"Yeah, I'm supposed to go straight home." Fred swung his backpack over his shoulder. "Did you see the yellow jackets at lunch? They were so cool."

Sam shook his head. "I was with the nurse. My adenoids were bugging me. But I heard they were scary."

Fred spotted a stick under a bush lining the walkway, grabbed it, and dragged it along a neighborhood fence. "Lisa jumped in the trashcan. When she got out, she was covered in chocolate pudding."

"I wish I could have seen that." Sam snorted.

A Rottweiler leapt hard against a gate, and both boys jumped back.

"That scared me. I hate dogs." Sam pressed his inhaler to his lips and puffed.

Fred lifted the stick in the air and tossed it over the fence. "Fetch boy." The mutt continued to growl and bark, clawing to get over.

"Let's go, Freddy." Sam took off running.

Fred stuck his tongue out at the dog and ran down the street. When they reached the end of the block, he asked, *"Want to come over for brownies? My aunt promised to make some."*

Sam fingered a short curl. *"Yeah, but I can't."*

"How come?"

"My dad wants me to do extra homework tonight. Said my spelling grade last week was bogus."

"You got a ninety-four percent."

"Yes, but he said it was six percent shy of perfect."

Fred pouted. From where he stood, Sam's dad was mean. He always made him work more and play less. Basically, he was the exterminator of fun. Fred had never been allowed over, and Sam was lucky if he got to hang out on Saturday. *"Okay. I guess I'll see you tomorrow."*

"Yeah, see you." Sam adjusted his backpack and continued down the street.

Fred turned for the blue door. The sweet, chocolaty smell of homemade brownies reached him from the moment his foot hit the first step. He licked his lips in anticipation.

"Auntie, I'm home." He dropped his backpack in the hall and kicked the door shut. *"I'll take mine with vanilla ice cream and—"* He stopped.

Aunt Tori lay on the couch face down, sobbing.

"Auntie, what's wrong?"

She didn't answer.

He shuffled closer. *"Auntie?"*

She pushed herself up, her eyes puffy, her nose red.

His stomach tightened.

"Honey, come sit next to me." She patted the flowered cushion and stuck out her hand to him.

He walked to the sofa and perched on the edge.

"A couple of Army officers were just here." She

49

sniffed and a new stream of tears started to flow, her voice almost inaudible. "They said your mother was found—" She gasped.

Something clutched his throat. The room tilted underneath him. His lungs struggled to be filled.

"Give me a minute," she whispered. "Go to your room, and I'll come see you in a moment."

Fred stared at her in a daze. Their eyes linked and she waved for him to go. What happened to my mom? "I'm not going anywhere. Tell me now!"

"Your mother missed you so much. She, uh..." She grabbed his hand. "Apparently, she left the base without permission. A truck driver found her..." A gurgle sound shot from her throat, sending a new onslaught of tears down her cheeks.

His chest ached from the pounding of his heart. He squeezed her hand, hoping she'd continue.

"They found her body on the side of the road."

He pulled away. "But she's okay, right? She's coming home soon?"

The new tears that followed answered his question. She shook her head and reached to pull him to her. "I'm so sorry."

Anger boiled in his chest. "No!" He jumped up and stomped his foot. "No, she's not dead. She's fine. She supposed to be home in a month." He started to cry. "She said she'd return before my birthday. She said we'd get a place and be together. She said this would fix everything. She said..." He crumpled to the floor at his aunt's feet. "She said..."

Tori slid down to the carpet and draped her arms over his head. "I know, hon. I know."

Chapter Eleven

"Mr. Avarice. Can I call you Lee?" Stan sat down in the yellow plastic chair by the bed and stretched out his legs. "What can you tell me that will bring a certain homicidal maniac to justice, huh?"

Fred turned from the mirror and walked toward the bed. He recognized the detective's expression. It was the face of loss. It started in the eyes and tugged at the skin. A look of weariness that turned the mouth down and hollowed the cheeks. "This isn't fair. I can see him, but he can't see me. How am I supposed to help him?"

Bill peered up from the book in his hand. "My guess is he's just as frustrated as you are. Maybe more."

Stan leaned forward and clasped his hands in front of him. "You see, Lee, there's this crazy person on the loose who has killed at least a dozen men that we know of." He stood up and started pacing, just missing Fred's knee. "Each victim falls in the same category as you. Wealthy moguls hated by all, married to their money and power. Your type, my friend, are dropping like diseased rodents to a serial psychopath."

He stopped and folded his arms. "Just this morning I was given a glimmer of hope." He laughed with a crumb of sarcasm. "I get a call from a friend of mine saying the first victim wasn't dead, and he's lying in a convalescent hospital downtown."

The cop hit the mattress, just missing the body's

leg. "I couldn't believe it. I had a live witness." He rolled his shoulders back and stuck out his chin. "So, I have this great morning. I get an espresso, which I don't do anymore. I stop and get a shave at the barber." He rubbed his cheek. "Haven't done that in years. But I'm floating on cloud nine. So forget my caffeine-free diet and the cost of a professional shave. I'm in a good mood. Why, you ask?" He stared at the bed for a moment; only the sounds of the equipment echoed in the quiet room. He knelt by the bed and whispered in the body's ear. "Because, Mr. Avarice, I was coming to talk to you. And with your help, I was going to catch the man who shot my father."

Fred glanced at Bill.

Stan's face contorted, and he rubbed his eyes with both hands. "Yep, that's right. The same guy, who shot you, probably shot my old man." He got up from the floor and sat back in the chair. "Of course, if the captain knew I was here, he'd be livid. I was pulled off the case the second he knew it was my dad who was shot." He wiped at his nose, his voice cracking. "I was on the case a total of thirty seconds. Long enough to park my car." Stan sighed. "He was number two. Funny, but my dad didn't even fit the profile. Analysis shows the weapon was the same. But he was a cop, and the other ten were business-men like you."

Heaviness weighed in Fred's mind. "Why can't I wake up and help this man?"

"You actually care about him?"

He shot Bill a look of disdain. "No, I want justice for my shooter."

Bill shook his head and grinned. "You can't wake up, because it's not your time yet."

He glared at his companion. "Who says, you crazy old coot?"

Bill's head bobbed side-to-side like a dog on a dashboard. He puffed his chest out and cusped his hands together. "Crazy old coot? Ha! I'm the only person who's willing to put up with you, Mr. Cantankerous Sourpuss." He poked his finger at Fred. "You spent all your time making money and now you have nothing to show for it. You want to go back? Then stop feeling sorry for yourself and figure out where you went wrong." He stepped back and crossed his arms. "And you can start making things right by giving me an apology."

Fred laughed. "Apology? I've never apologized to anyone in my life." He stared at the ceiling and smiled. "Hey, I remember that."

"Well, whooptee doopty doo. Good for you. Now where's my sorry?"

"I just told you, I don't do that."

The old man's eyes narrowed. "And I'm telling you that if you can't start by telling a nice elderly gentleman you're sorry, how in the world do you expect to change?"

"Remember the Fonz would stutter when he'd try to say sorry?"

Bill stared at him as if roaches were climbing out of his nose. "The who?"

"The Fonz. Arthur Fonzerelli. From *Happy Days*."

His face remained blank.

"You never saw *Happy Days*?"

Bill flipped around and looked to the far corner. His hands shook as he pointed. "Oh no, it can't be."

"What? What do you see?"

"A dark spot."

Fred followed his gaze. "You do not."

Bill pointed. "Yeah, right there. Don't you see it?"

"Maybe it's here for you." Fred smirked.

"No, not possible." Bill grabbed Fred by the sleeve. "It's been nice knowing you."

Fred squinted. "I don't see anything."

"Are you blind as well as comatose?"

"That's the second time you've pulled that on me. I'm not buying it."

"No, need to buy it." Bill smiled. "Hell is free."

Fred batted the air. "I wasn't bad enough to go to Hell."

Bill found his stool and propped one knee on top of it. "Trust me, you wrote the book on bad."

"No, I self-published a book on money management."

He shook his head. "You're boring *and* stupid."

"Hey, I remembered my book. This is wonderful."

The detective got up from his seat and placed the notebook in his jacket. "Well, Mr. Avarice, it's been stimulating, but I'd better go before I'm missed at work." He patted the body's leg once and left.

Fred followed him to the door, threw up his hands, and let out a whiny moan. "Ugh! If only I could wake up so I could tell him who did it."

Bill mounted his stool as if it was a saddle on a horse and rolled around the room. "Fred—D."

Fred watched the man slide from one side of the room to the other. "Can you please stop that? You're making me dizzy, and you're wasting time."

The old man waved his arms in the air like a cowboy at a rodeo. "You want to know the one thing

I've learned hanging out with you coma dupes?"

"What's that?"

"There's one thing you have lots of and that's time, my friend. Time." Bill ran his stool into the wall and kicked back, causing him to almost flip over. "When you've got lots of time to squander, you've got to think of creative ways to entertain yourself. If you don't, you'll go mad."

"Too late for you, I guess."

"Ha! Good one," Bill guffawed. "Now, about the meaning behind my grand wise words."

"Oh brother."

"You want to wake up? Figure out what could have prevented this in the first place." He pushed off and landed with a crash into Fred's calves.

"Ouch! Okay, I've had enough companionship, old man. Go back to wherever you came from. I'm fine here by myself. I don't need anything from you."

"What?" Bill walked to the bed and hovered over the body. "You think he's going to wake up without a miracle?"

"I've got willpower. That has brought me through more than you can desire. I've never needed anyone in my life. If that's how I'm to die, then so be it. But if I want to wake up, then I'll wake up."

"Fine, go ahead. Wake up." Bill motioned for Fred to come stand next to the body. "Go on, all powerful Freddy. Make yourself come out of a coma. Follow your dream."

Fred wasn't about to be made a fool by some wisecracking, old man. He stepped next to the bed and positioned himself on top of his body. He closed his eyes. *I want to wake up. I'm going to wake up. Wake up.*

"Wake up! Wake up!" He opened his eyes and sat up, but his body didn't follow. "I guess I'm just not in the mood right now. I'll do it later."

"Wake up. Wake up." Bill mimicked, then held his stomach laughing, hysterical. "That was one of my life's most classic moments. Wake up. Wake up. Oh, stop making me laugh. You're going to kill me." He wiped under his eyes and looked like he might stop laughing, but then started snickering again. Then doubled over in a fit of laughter. "Wake up. Wake up."

"Glad I could be so entertaining." He walked away from the body and started to pace. "I need to get out of here. I'm trapped."

Bill stepped in line behind Fred, pacing with him.

"There must be a reason I'm going through all of this."

"I follow you."

Fred scratched his chin. "There's got to be meaning to this coma."

Bill imitated scratching his chin. "I understand."

Fred flipped around and pointed at Bill. "You're not helping."

"The answer is simple. A kindergartner could figure it out."

"Oh really. And what's that?"

Bill pointed at the mirror. "Go back in. Only an earnest look at who you are will help you find the answers you've been searching for."

"Aw yes, Billy-san." Fred bowed and moved to the mirror. This time, he knew where he would go, and that frightened him.

Chapter Twelve

The house laid just ahead, its windows mocking him with ridicule. Today had been a pretty good day until the police got involved.

What time is it? *Fred checked his watch. 4:00 p.m. Two hours before his aunt would get home from work. Maybe he could think of a suitable excuse by then. Even better yet, maybe she wouldn't know. Yeah, there was a chance the school hadn't called. He squared his shoulders and trudged up the steps of the two-story townhouse.*

Opening the door, he decided to play it coy. To pretend he didn't know what he'd done was wrong. Maybe pretend to be shocked. He unlocked the front door, tossed his backpack in the closet, and went into the kitchen. Rummaging through the fridge, he grabbed a can of cream soda and some day-old pizza, before climbing the stairs to his room.

He slammed the door, cranked the Police's newest album on his new tape player, and pigged out while the setting sun brought his fate closer to the present. At ten minutes to six, he heard the front door open. His stomach turned his afternoon snack over in anticipation. He didn't have to wait long. Within minutes, he heard feet on the stairs.

"Freddy, get out here!" Yep, his aunt sounded furious.

He stared across the dim room at a Fleetwood Mac poster on his wall and gulped. He knew why she wanted to talk to him, but he still wasn't ready. He needed more time to think, to create a better excuse than denial. He closed his eyes. Who am I kidding? *There wasn't one. He was in a deep dumpster.*

"Freddy!" His aunt flung open the door and flipped on the light, her face red, eyes aflame. "What are you doing in the dark? I've been calling you."

"I couldn't hear you." He sat up, rubbing his eyes and yawning. "I was taking a nap."

She turned off the stereo and placed her hands on her waist. "I guess you know who called me at work today, or you wouldn't be up here hiding."

He averted his eyes.

"What were you thinking? "

His tongue froze. No response.

"Freddy, look at me. You could go to jail."

Fred met her stare. "I did it for you."

Her eyes narrowed. "Oh no you don't. You're not going to give me another lame excuse about not wanting me to end up like your mom." She stepped closer to where he lay on the bed. "Have you ever missed a meal?"

He didn't answer.

"Answer me. In the last five years, have you ever gone hungry?"

He felt stupid answering. "No."

"Have you ever gone to school naked or in rags?"

He rolled his eyes.

"Well, have you?"

"Of course not."

"How about at school? Ever missed out on

anything there?"

"No!" She was starting to really bug him. "I know what you're doing." He stared back at the poster and allowed his eyes to glaze over, Stevie blurring into a smeared gray image.

"My point is we're not penniless. You haven't gone without anything under my roof. So, why do you have this insatiable urge to make money?" She sat on the corner of his bed and sighed. "Freddy, I love you. I have always been happy I took you in. You are like my son." She touched his hands. "But if you keep doing things like this..."

He snapped his neck to face her.

"I'm going to have to find another place for you to stay."

"What?" He felt ill. "So, you'd just throw me away? Just like that."

Her head shook side-to-side, sending her hair clip into her lap. Her blonde locks tumbled around her shoulders. She snatched up the barrette and met his gaze. "No, not just like that. It would never be that easy." She grabbed his shoulder. "But I won't have you performing illegal business deals in my home, either. If you want to stay here, then you'll get it together. If you want money so bad, go work at Burger Barn. Stop trying to con people out of their lunch money with trick die."

"You know about the dice?"

"Yes." She reached into the pocket of her powder-blue cardigan and withdrew a tissue. "I'm tired of getting calls from the principal. This time, the police are involved."

That wasn't a surprise. "I know. Krissy's dad is a

cop."

"And I'm guessing you made a killing off her."

He tried not to smile. "Forty dollars."

"Freddy!" Her mouth swung open. "That's insane. Did she pay you?"

He reached under his pillow and pulled a wad of ones. "Yep." He smiled at the victory in his hand.

His aunt reached for the money, but he recoiled. "I worked for this."

"No, you stole that money, and you will give it back at once."

"No, I won't." He swung his legs over the side of the mattress and stood.

She flipped around and joined him on the other side of the bed. "You will, or you'll be out of my house."

The two of them glared at one another, neither budging. He imagined "Riders in the Sky" playing in the background. It would come down to who was more stubborn. A honk in the driveway broke their stare.

Fred glanced out the window. His soon-to-be uncle *had arrived for a date. "Better go. Wouldn't want to leave Uncle Bobby waiting for you."*

She pointed her finger at Fred and opened her mouth to say something, but seemed to redirect. "Fine, but we'll finish this conversation tomorrow." She turned to go. "In the meantime, you're on restriction. No TV, phone, or friends." With that, she was gone.

Restriction? Forget that. *Fred flung open his closet door and reached behind his clothes. Anger clouded his vision, so he relied on touch. His fingers grazed what felt like canvas and he yanked. A green duffel bag fell out onto the floor in front of him.*

Who does she think she is anyway? She's not my mother. *He breathed out through his nose and shook his head. No matter what she thought of him, he did it for her.*

He reached in the closet again and pulled out a metal Partridge Family lunchbox. He carried it to his bed and popped open the lid. Over five years of savings filled the tin. He added the wad from the day and snapped it closed.

He turned for the closet again, enclosed his arms around the hanging clothes, and pulled. The outfits were heavier than he thought and he fell, toppled by piles of clothes.

"Crud!" He scooted back and shoved the outfits aside. Maybe I shouldn't try to take everything. Just the things I'll miss. *He pulled out one suit, a couple sweaters, and a nice shirt. If he planned to be a business entrepreneur, he would need the nicest clothes he owned.*

The rest of his clothes he left on the floor. He walked to his dresser and pulled out a week's worth of socks, underwear, T-shirts, and jeans, along with three nice pairs of pants. He stuffed them into the duffel bag. He grabbed toiletries from the bathroom, a couple Star Wars books from the living-room bookshelf, and the picture of his mom from his dresser. Once he had his bounty, he tossed them in and zipped the bag closed. He lifted the strap over his shoulder and tucked the lunch box under his arm. He was ready.

Wait. He set the duffel bag down and stepped out into the hallway. The hall closet held several sleeping bags. Just in case. *He grabbed one and returned to retrieve his bag.*

Now he was ready. When his aunt returned, she'd have her wish. He'd be gone and out of her life—for good.

****

The sun peeked behind the horizon, causing a chill to fall over the city. Fred spotted the orange house a block away. On his first visit, his best friend, Sam had told him he couldn't miss it, and he was right. It reminded him of a salmon salad his mom used to make every Christmas. He grimaced at the memory of his mom making him bring the foul concoction to his lips. The mushy carrot-colored gelatin smelled of day-old fish and sour mayonnaise. The motion to swallow the bite lent to a ten-second trip to the porcelain altar.

Now facing the front door of his friend's house, he questioned whether he should knock or go around to Sam's window? If he knocked, he might risk being sent home. Creeping along the hedges, he peered between the blinds in each room. When he got to the last window on the west side, he spotted a poster of Farrah Fawcett on the wall. Sam's room.

There was a thick bush blocking Fred's ability to tap on the glass, so he reached to the dirt by his feet and tossed a few wood chips. Nothing. He tried again. This time, the blinds moved. He waved, and the window-coverings lifted.

"What are you doing here? I'm doing homework," Sam said.

"I ran away from home." Fred moved as close as he could. "I need a place to crash for the night."

Sam glanced over his shoulder and then back out the window. "If I let you in here, my old man will have my skin. He's still mad about the dice."

"Why do you think I'm here?"

The red-haired guy looked at the bags at Fred's feet and shook his head. "It can't be that bad."

"Trust me, it is."

"Well, if I help you, we'll both be looking for shelter." He leaned back in and moved to shut the window. "Sorry, Freddy. Really I am." The blinds closed, as did his plan.

Now what? Fred lifted his duffel bag and turned to go. Sam was the only friend he had. The truth was Fred wasn't even close to being popular. When people looked in their yearbook they would say, "Oh, yeah, that's the guy who scammed me."

A grumble from his stomach cut through the night. Well, he had money; it wasn't as if he was a vagrant. Maybe he could get a hotel and figure things out from there. His sixteenth birthday was in two days, so hopefully, he could get a job. In the meantime, he'd have to live off his savings.

A few miles down the block, he spotted a vacancy sign at the Blue Genie Motel. This looked like the kind of place that would take cash only. But his age might be an issue. Chances were pretty high they wouldn't rent to a minor, so his conning-skills would have to be first rate.

"Can I help you?" the elderly man said from his seat behind the counter.

"Yes, I was wondering if my Uncle Jack has checked in yet." Fred glanced at the digital watch on his wrist. "He said he'd be here by 3:00 p.m."

The man looked down at his book. "His last name?"

"Baton."

He scaled the page with his finger. When he reached the bottom, he looked up and shook his head. "No Baton. Sorry."

Fred let out a deep sigh and sat down on his duffel bag. "That's so like him to be late. Knowing him, he'll roll in around two in the morning." He glanced back at the man. "Hey, would you mind if I hang out here until he comes?"

The scowl on the man's face said he didn't seem too excited about the idea.

"Of course, he gave me the money. If you want, I could pay for the room, and you could send him over when he gets here."

The man stared at him for a moment.

Freddy didn't flinch.

"Do you have a credit card? We need one to hold the room."

Fred got up and slapped a $100 bill on the counter. "How about I leave this as a deposit? My uncle doesn't believe in plastic. Just pays more up front. He likes this kind of no-tell motel, if you know what I mean. Work for you?"

The man licked his lips and reached for the bill. "Works for me." He wrote Jack Baton in the book and handed Fred a key with blue plastic tag. "Your room is on the end, upstairs."

"Thanks." Fred glanced at the key in his hand, gathered his stuff, and set off for his room. He set his bag by the door and unlocked the knob. A smile broke on his face at the reality of his accomplishment. One mental pat on the back. The art of deception is a powerful tool.

Once inside, he cranked up the air conditioner,

flipped on the TV, and ordered pizza from the first restaurant listed. Within an hour, he was fed, bathed, and ready to take on a new life.

****

The next morning, a call from the front desk woke him up. "You asked to be called at seven, sir?"

"Yes, thank you." Fred hung up the receiver and climbed out of bed. Within a few minutes, he was dressed and ready to go. He glanced over at his bags and frowned. He couldn't very well take them to school; he'd need another plan. Wait! What am I thinking? *He couldn't return to school now, could he? If he did, his aunt would claim him for sure. A wave of sadness washed over him. He would miss her…and Sam.*

His stomach ached. The truth made it hurt more. I don't think I can do this. *When it came down to the truth, though, it wasn't his aunt or Sam he missed. It was his mom. He squared his shoulders.* Can't lose faith and get sappy. *He had to be strong. Today was a new adventure. He would use the day to find a permanent place to stay and search for a job. He knew how. After all, he followed his mom doing both for years.*

The open door brought intense light, contrasting the dark room. He squinted as he grabbed his bags and set out.

On the corner, he spotted a coffee shop. The smell of sugar frosting and fresh-baked dough filled the air. He pointed to a maple-crème bar and chocolate milk in the case. He was about to hand the lady the money, when he spotted a newspaper on a stand to his left. "I'll take one of those, too."

"One-seventy-five," she said.

65

He handed her the money, stuffed the paper under his arm, the donut in his mouth, grabbed the milk, and walked down the street. The park was a few blocks away, close enough to make it on foot. Once there, he found a secluded piece of shaded grass and sat to enjoy his breakfast. Except for a couple kissing on a bench nearby, the park was empty.

He bit into his donut. Custard oozed out and dripped down his chin. He wiped it off and then licked his finger. A brown and yellow bird flapped down next to his leg and pecked at the ground. Fred pulled off a crumb and tossed it a few inches from where it stood. The bird's head swiveled side to side, and then it hopped to the crumb. Fred smiled and turned to the newspaper. He flipped the pages until he reached the "want ads." The crinkling paper must have frightened the bird. It flapped into the air and was gone.

Fred shrugged and scanned the top page. A big black square stood out with the words, "Help wanted. Make lots of money fast. No experience necessary." Cool, works for me.

Chapter Thirteen

Fred blinked. Once again, he stood in the hospital room. A soft murmur came from behind the curtain. He turned away from the mirror and walked toward the sound.

"Stop! Don't go in there." Bill stood behind him, his arm out like a traffic cop.

"Why not?"

"Trust me." He flipped around him, shaking his head. "It's not pretty."

Fred reached out a hand.

"Stop." Bill almost fell trying to stop him.

"Tell me why. Who's over there?"

Bill rubbed a hand over his head. "Who said anyone is over there?"

"The nurse always goes back there. I assume to wait on another patient."

"Yes, that may very well be. But I assure you, you don't want to see whoever is there."

"Come on."

"Have I led you wrong yet?"

Fred cocked his head to the side. "I don't know. Do you see spots?"

"Touché." Bill encircled Fred's shoulders with his right arm and led him back to the mirror. "Let's return to your happy childhood. It's so fun."

"Right. Look, I don't think I can take anymore of

traipsing down memory lane. It's kind of lame."

"As was your life, my friend."

Fred narrowed his eyes. "You don't know me or my life. You've seen a minuscule portion. Not enough to judge me."

The old man sat next to the body and pretended to tickle his feet. "I've seen enough to know you're a big mess. Goochy goochy goo."

"Stop that."

Bill smirked. "Why should I? You can't feel it anyway. And it amuses me. Ticky, ticky, ticky."

Fred walked to Bill's side and slapped his hand away from the body. "It's stupid and a waste of time."

"You honestly don't get this whole coma thing, do you? You've got all the time the universe has to offer. You might as well find ways to entertain yourself." Bill snapped his fingers. "I know…how about you think of some exotic destination and then take me along. I've always wanted to go to…" Bill's eyes glazed over and he sighed. "Kansas."

Fred rolled his eyes. "Kansas is hardly exotic. Don't you mean the Bahamas? Tahiti? Maybe the Caribbean? I've always wanted to go there."

"Not everything exciting is found in the sun, my man. Besides, that's boring. Sitting on the beach, sleeping with a drink in your hand? Oh yeah, that's real stimulating." He batted at the air. "I can do that here."

"You're a spirit. Why not take off and go to Kansas then? You can leave me in peace and do whatever it is a tourist does in Kansas." Fred placed a hand on his chin. "Do they even have a tourist board in Kansas? You know, maybe to tell everyone how their state got so flat."

"Ha." Bill stuck out his tongue and pretended to slap the body. "I'll have you know Laura Ingalls Wilder's house is in Kansas."

"The *Little House on the Prairie* girl? Ooh." Fred rolled his eyes. "I stand corrected. Very exotic."

"Back to the mirror with you, buddy." Bill pointed across the room. "It's obvious you still need a plethora of work done."

"Meandering down memory lane isn't going to change the fact I'm in a coma." Fred folded his arms and shook his head. "I can't change the past, old man. Face it, I'm stuck in this world with a bullet in my brain and the inability to wake up on my own." He motioned to the body's head. "Look at me. I'm Rip Van Winkle." He slumped to the floor, weary. "I'm going to live in this room with you forever."

"Forever, forever, forever..." Bill echoed.

"Okay, enough."

"No, not enough. Forever and ever and ever—"

"Bill, *please*."

"It's not forever anyway. Only until that black shadow gets you." Bill nodded to the corner. "And who knows, that could be sooner rather than later."

"Stop with the shadow thing. I know there is no shadow. So, you can knock that off, too."

The crazy coot reached under the bed and revealed a small box filled with tongue suppressors and cotton balls. "Let's play checkers. Since you're all soft inside with no back bone, you can be the cotton balls."

"What's that supposed to mean?"

The old man knelt on the floor and began placing cotton balls and sticks on the individual tiles. "It means I don't know how you ended up rich. You're not much of a risk taker. Someone who isn't afraid to step out in faith and see what just might be. Instead, what I see is a chicken afraid of his own shadow."

"Are you talking about shadows again?"

Bill looked up from his preparation and shook his head. "Another reason I can't believe you're so successful. You're kind of a nitwit."

"Okay, enough. I don't want you to be my companion anymore." Fred pivoted on his heel. "I want to be left alone for the duration of my stay."

"Nope, not leaving." Bill pointed to the floor. "It's your turn. Move your ball."

Cotton balls lined the floor by the door and sticks mirrored them by the curtain. "Maybe I'm not in the mood to play a game with you."

"Do you prefer moping and feeling sorry for yourself? Because that is way more useful."

Fred stared at him for a moment. He had a point. "Fine. I guess it is a bit ingenious."

Bill bowed with an arm in front and an arm behind. "Thank you. Thank you very much."

Fred sighed and pushed a ball with his foot diagonally to the tile next to him. "We don't have far to go before we end up under the bed."

"Makes it more exciting, doesn't it?"

Bill moved his stick to the left and Fred matched his move on the right. "Why'd you call me a chicken?"

Bill jumped one of Fred's cotton balls, picked it up, and stuffed it in his pocket. "Your only hope is to understand your life. It's a simple task. And yet, you're afraid of your own reflection. It's a bit cowardly, don't you think?"

"No, because searching inside one's self is the

scariest thing of all. Most people are afraid to admit that maybe they aren't smart enough, good enough, pretty enough." Fred pushed another ball. "That's why people run away, screaming from the second gate."

Bill looked up. "Huh? What gate?"

"The discussion just reminded me of a childhood movie."

"Never saw any picture show. What's it about?"

"It's about the loss of children reading. A warrior-child has to go on a journey through Fantasia to get another kid to read his story."

"You've lost me, but continue."

"Well, one of the places the warrior must visit is the all-knowing Oracle. To get to her, people have to pass through two gates. The first one is a big sphinx that shoots lasers at anyone who isn't brave. The second is a mirror. According to the movie, most people 'when faced with their true selves run away screaming'."

"I see." Bill went back to jumping cotton balls. "Look, I win."

Fred glanced around the room. Sure enough, big ice cream sticks covered the floor. Not one cotton ball remained. "I supposed you did."

Bill rested cross-legged in the middle of the room, playing with his spoils of cotton. "What happened to you when you ran away from home? Did you make it on your own?"

Fred thought about that for a moment, but as before, his memory was fuzzy. "I don't know."

"Most street urchins don't work in a place that would give them enough money to afford this place. You must have had a stroke of luck somewhere."

"Yeah, I must have." He sighed and moved to the

mirror again. He did want answers, and it was obvious he would have to endure painful memories to achieve them. His reflection still gone from the mirror, he stared into the silver glass with wide eyes, afraid of where it might take him next.

Chapter Fourteen

"Mr. Fenton will see you now," the receptionist said.

Lee stood and walked through the open double doors. A tall man with a well-trimmed beard and glasses greeted him with a handshake and motioned for him to sit at the end of the conference table.

Lee sat.

"Do you have your application?"

Working to steady his trembling hand, he slid the paper to the man and then folded a fist into his lap. Just breathe.

Mr. Fenton studied the application with a stony expression. When his eyes reached the bottom, he lowered the page. "You're only sixteen, Fredrick?"

"I go by my middle name, Lee, now." He cleared his throat. "And yes, sir. I'm sixteen."

"And you have no experience outside of working at your high school snack bar?"

"Well, I mowed lawns for a summer, but I didn't think that would count."

"Hmm." The man's mouth puckered as if he planned to kiss the form in his hand. Instead, he set it down and said, "I think I'll give you a try." He pivoted around in his chair and pulled a document off the shelf behind him. "First thing you need to understand is that we have the strictest confidentiality here. You must sign

a waiver. Are you okay with that?"

Lee shrugged. "Sure."

"Good." He placed a document on a clipboard and slid it and a pen across to Lee. "Welcome to Melton and Gray."

Chapter Fifteen

Stan sat on the floor of his living room with his legs under the coffee table, eating overcooked frozen pizza, staring at a photo of his family.

The cell rang from the kitchen counter. He scooted back and grabbed the phone. "Hello?"

"What time are you coming in?" Bogan asked.

He glanced at the clock. *Wow, that late already?* "I'll be in shortly. Why? What's up?"

She exhaled into the phone. "I don't know how to tell you this—"

"Just say it."

"O'Dell spotted your sister at the Senator's Ball last week. She was draped on the arm of some mafia type, but took off when she saw O'Dell."

His sister? Stan's heart skipped. He looked back at the family picture. It was an Easter picture from when they were kids. Her hair was pulled up, and she wore a bonnet with a daisy almost the size of her face, clutching a chocolate rabbit in her hand. It was bad enough losing his father, but she wasn't even around to help him work through the grief. She ran away from home years ago and didn't even know their dad was dead.

He leaned his elbows on the counter. "Do we know who the goon is?"

"We're working on it." She let out a slight giggle.

"Well, O'Dell is working on it."

"Tell O'Dell thanks."

"No bother. You know he'd do anything for you."

She was right. O'Dell had been his father's partner for years. Stan rolled his neck from left to right. "I'll be in soon."

"Okay, see you."

"Bye. And thanks." He hung up the phone and returned to the picture he held in his hand. She was cute and so smart. If only their mother hadn't passed away so suddenly, maybe his sister would have turned out all right.

****

Lee stood in the hall outside the big boss's office door shifting from one foot to the other. From inside, he could hear his immediate supervisor, Jake, ready to complain. "Excuse me, sir, I hate to bother you, but—"

"Then don't," Melton said.

"But, sir, there's a kid in your mailroom who has become a problem."

"Kent, why are you bringing this to me? Take it to Fenton. He runs the mailroom issues."

"No, sir, it's not that kind of trouble. It's about things." His voice lowered.

Lee leaned forward, straining to hear.

"What's his name, and what does he know?"

Kent cleared his throat. "His name is Lee Avarice. I'm not sure how much he knows; only that he was giving a couple of your brokers strategy tips on manipulating customers."

"Which brokers?"

"Finch and Anderson."

"Bring the kid here."

"He's actually in the hall."

Lee straightened up and diverted his stare down the hall. A slender woman made her way toward him, heels clicking on the marble floor.

The door opened, but the woman blocked his supervisor's path. She pushed past him. "Hi, honey. I came by to give you the name you wanted."

"You could have done that over the phone, Krystal. I'm busy."

She didn't close the door, and Lee could see through to his big desk.

"Fine." She tossed a manila file on the desk, knocking his pencil cup on the floor, then kissed his cheek. "See you at home."

Melton scowled and reached for his cup. "Don't come down here again."

She flipped her hair over her shoulder and sauntered out. Melton's gaze followed her exit, his eyes landing on Lee. "Come in, Mr. Avarice."

Lee shuffled forward. "Hello, sir." He didn't approach Melton's desk, instead he stood by the door with his hands fidgeting at his side.

Melton rose from his chair. "I won't bite, Mr. Avarice. Come closer so we can talk."

The young man stepped forward and stood within ten inches of the mahogany desk. Melton looked him over. Lee could see his reflection in the window. His long dark hair was slicked back and banded in a ponytail. His white shirt was pressed and his khaki pants appeared clean and tidy, his firm jaw shaved and a pair of glasses sat high on his nose. What is this man staring at?

"Please sit." Melton motioned to the high-backed

leather chair positioned to the right of his desk.

Avarice looked at the chair, back to Melton, and then moved to sit.

The burly man came around the desk and sat on the corner facing the chair. "You've been with Melton and Gray for almost three years. Am I right?"

"Yes, sir."

"And Fenton tells me you're a good worker."

Lee half-grinned. "Thank you, sir."

"It's been brought to my attention that you've been talking to my brokers about misleading my customers."

Avarice swallowed. "I'm sorry, sir. I just overheard them discussing some problems in the elevator. I offered them a suggestion."

Melton pressed his lips together and nodded. "I see. And what is it you overheard?"

The young man studied his hands. "How to con some lady out of her inheritance."

"And you offered them some advice?"

He met Melton's gaze. "I know I shouldn't have said anything. I just blurted out the first thing that came to mind."

"I see." Melton walked back around his desk and opened a red folder. "Your real name is Fredrick. Why do you go by Lee?"

"Am I in trouble, sir?"

He grinned. "That all depends."

"On what, sir?"

"On whether or not you're honest with me." He reached into his drawer and withdrew a bottle of scotch and two tumblers. "Drink?"

Avarice shook his head.

"I guess you're not really old enough, are you?"

Melton shrugged and poured himself a glass. "I'm a powerful man, Mr. Avarice. I know more than you can conceive. So, it would be within your best interest to level with me. When I ask a question, I expect an answer." He leaned in. "The right one."

Avarice sighed. "I ran away from home a few days before my sixteenth birthday. I used my middle name in order to keep my aunt from finding me. I figured if she was asking around for Freddy, no one would think of me."

"Very good." Melton shot the amber liquid back into his throat and swallowed. "Tell me what you told the men in the elevator."

Avarice shifted in seat. "I told them the key to any con is building trust."

Melton raised an eyebrow. "And how would you know that, Mr. Avarice?"

"I...um..." He cleared his throat. "I used to con people out of money in high school. It's how I was able to run away when I did."

"I see." Melton poured himself another drink. "And how much money were you able to con from your friends?"

"It took me about five years, but my final amount was four thousand, five hundred eighty-two dollars." Lee smiled. "And twenty-seven cents."

Melton leaned forward. "That's almost a hundred a month. Not a bad plunder. I'm impressed." He tapped the red folder on his forearm and the opened it. "Fredrick Lee Avarice. Born in 1965. Orphaned by age ten. Lived with your aunt until you ran away at age fifteen. Got in trouble a few times for fraud, and then turned up at Melton and Gray Brokerage Firm."

"You already knew all that?"

The big man's eyes bore into his. "Tell me, Mr. Avarice, how would you like a promotion?"

He peered side to side, surprised. "Me?"

"I'm about to reveal something to you. But before I do, you're going to need to sign a contract for me." Melton pushed the intercom on his phone. "Miss Myers, please bring an H.E.L. contract to me."

"Yes, sir."

He turned back to Avarice. "I need an answer. Do you want to be promoted?"

"Well, I know I don't want to stay in the mailroom forever." Lee rubbed his hands together and nodded once. "So, yeah. I guess so."

The door opened and his secretary entered with a carbon paper document. She set it on the corner of the desk in front of Avarice.

"Thank you, Miss Myers. You may go."

She nodded and left the room.

"What is minimum wage now? Three twenty-five?" Melton asked.

Lee shifted. "Two sixty-five."

"Well, for a man with your talents, I think you're going to like this raise." He pulled a gold pen from his lapel. "I need you to sign this form, stating you will never disclose what we do here at Melton and Gray. It also states we're in partnership together and should you branch out, you will owe me a portion of your profits until you reach the sum here." He pointed to a line item. "In about a year, you're looking at about fifty-K annually." He held out the pen. "Sound good? Or would you rather return to your two sixty-five in the mailroom?"

A big smile flashed across Lee's face. He grabbed the pen and scooted forward. "Where do I sign?"

Melton pointed to the bottom of the paper. "Right here." He leaned back. "I'm anxious to see your potential, kid."

He slid the signed form across the desk and smiled. "Thank you for this opportunity."

"Don't thank me yet." Melton placed the paper in the red folder and closed it. "I'll need you to go to training. Can you leave on Thursday?"

"Sure."

"Good. I'll have Fenton make the arrangements." Melton stood and pointed to the door. "You can go back to work."

Lee stood. "Thank you again, Mr. Melton."

"You're welcome."

Lee hurried out the door, but not before hearing him hit the intercom and say, "Take care of Finch and Anderson."

Chapter Sixteen

Stan sat at his desk with his feet propped up. The custodian, James stood to the right of him with a broom in one hand and a rubber-band gun in the other.

"I wouldn't do that if I were you."

James let it fly.

Stan reached out and caught the band only millimeters from his ear. He turned to the custodian and glared.

The young man grinned and bolted down the hall.

Stan grunted.

"You shouldn't be so mean. He's trying to be your friend," Bogan said from behind him.

Stan kicked his feet to the floor and twisted around in his seat. The African-American woman looked striking in a plum cocktail dress that hugged her shape. He let out a low whistle. "Going somewhere, Officer Bogan?"

She fingered her glistening cropped curls and smiled. "Yeah, as a matter of fact I am."

"Big date?"

"Ha! Aren't you funny?" She slapped his shoulder playfully. "No, Santos and Wilson are trying to nab another pervert in the Gaslamp District. I agreed to help if they'd take *us* out for drinks later."

"Now, who's funny? You know I don't drink."

"It's not about you drinking. Have a cola for all I

care. It's about you getting out more." She touched his chin and smiled. "Away from thinking about the past."

It hurt to smile, so he looked away instead. "I'm not ready."

"You've been saying that for months. George isn't coming back, Heller." She picked up the Easter picture on his desk. "Neither is your sister."

He spun in his chair and grimaced. "Don't say that."

Her hands lifted in truce. "Sorry, I didn't mean to hurt you. I just meant that your sister has been missing for years."

"But you said O'Dell saw her."

"Yes, but I also said she took off. She obviously doesn't want to be found." She touched his shoulder. "So stop."

He cupped his hands around his face. Loneliness consumed him. Every day he woke up feeling like the orphan he was. "You better get going." He forced a grin. "You wouldn't want to miss your trick."

She kissed two of her fingers and touched them to his cheek. "I'm here if you need me."

"Thanks."

Her heels echoed down the hall and out the front door.

He wiped at his cheek and looked at the burgundy mark on his left hand. *Lipstick. That woman is incorrigible.* He reached for a tissue and rubbed his face again. For a second, he closed his eyes.

"Detective Heller?"

His head shot up. Captain Moses scowled at him from his office doorway. Stan swallowed. "Sir?"

"Are you getting paid to sleep?"

"Actually, I was praying, sir."

The heavyset man blew through his lips, reminding Stan of a horse. "Oh brother. Well, you'd better start praying for protection over your backside, because I'm about to put my boot into it."

Stan cleared his throat. "Sorry, sir. What can I do for you?"

The captain stepped forward. "For an appetizer, you can start by telling me if the rumors are true?"

"Rumors?"

Moses placed his pudgy fingers on the edge of Stan's desk and leaned forward. "You've been working on the tycoon murders despite my orders, haven't you?"

The smell of delicatessen onions and sweat permeated Stan's nostrils. He cringed. "No, sir. Not really."

The captain shot his head back and laughed. "Not really, he says." His face turned somber. "Are you, or aren't you?"

What could he say? No answer would suffice. Stan wiped his forehead. "He was my dad, sir. I haven't spent any company time investigating, but I've done a little digging on my time off. Nothing too serious."

"I'll be the judge of that." He pointed across the room to the office brown-noser. "Whatever you've found out, give it to Kessler. Then leave it alone. You're not authorized to be on that case."

"My dad wasn't a tycoon. Just an undercover cop—"

"To Kessler! Understood?"

Adrenaline pumped through Stan's veins. "Yes, sir."

"Good, now get going. You should have been off

the clock by now."

Stan snatched his jacket from the back of his chair and rushed down the hall. He sensed the captain's eyes on his back. Rage boiled Stan's blood, blurring his vision. He wanted to fight for justice, and he wasn't allowed to, simply because he was related to one of the victims. Stan pushed through a group of guys at the door, acknowledging them with a simple nod.

He climbed in his black Jeep and cranked on the radio. He didn't really want to go home, and he most certainly didn't want to go out. He placed the keys in the ignition and pulled out onto the busy road. He knew where he needed to be. The only place left with an ounce of hope.

****

Lee sat in the training room, fighting sleep. His eyes burned, and he yawned for probably the twentieth time. The five men around him fidgeted in their seats. It was well after midnight, and the group of trainees was tired from hours of learning about stock trading and mastering the ultimate con. They were all scheduled to fly out in the morning to different parts of the country. Their orders were simple—glean as much information as they could before that time.

"Are you getting any of this?" a man whispered behind him.

"Yeah, in the first eight hours maybe."

The bearded man in the front of the room turned on the projector and a diagram appeared on the screen. "The stops are the amount of money that you plan to take in the end. Think of it as a key to finish." The man pulled out another transparency and replaced it with the one on the glass. "Okay, I've given you all the facts; now let's look at a few examples. Mr. Smith invests ten thousand dollars. Melton and Gray covers you with a growth of thirty thousand. This will convince Mr. Smith that investing with us is lucrative. So, he'll invest more and the stocks will plummet. It is imperative—"

Mr. Melton stepped into the room. Lee and the other men straightened. The teacher stopped and walked over to him. Melton whispered in the man's ear. The teacher nodded, and Melton exited.

"Well, gentlemen. It looks like you're ready to go. Grab your cards, keys, and cases at the door. To your fortitude and success. Don't let us down."

****

Fred opened his eyes and turned from the mirror, just in time to see the door to his convalescent room open. The detective walked in with hunched shoulders and a downcast expression.

"He looks sad." Fred stepped away from his memory box and took a seat on the floor next to Bill. His companion was surprisingly docile leaning against the wall by the bed. "What do you suppose he wants today?"

Bill didn't answer; instead, he shut his eyes and murmured softly.

"You okay?"

Silence.

Is he praying?

"Well, Mr. Avarice, it seems I'm not supposed to take your case after all. I guess it isn't God's will for me to find out who did this to you. Can't say I'm not bummed." Stan flipped the chair around, straddled the seat, and rested his arms on the back. "I know there is a connection between my father's death and your shooting. But I guess I'll never know." The door opened, and he looked over his shoulder. "Nurse Jensen, good evening."

She smiled through a yawn. "Sorry, it's been a long day. Speaking of that, Detective, how'd you get in here? Visiting hours were over a while ago."

"Why, with my charming ways and astonishing good looks." He winked.

Her cheeks flushed. "You must have sweet-talked Nurse Higgins. Widowed for over twenty years, she'd fall for any line you'd give her."

"I counted on that."

"Oh brother. Those two really need to get together," Fred said, turning to Bill. "They're obviously flirting."

Bill still didn't respond.

"Bill?" *What's wrong with him? Usually, he looks for the chance to say a snide remark.* "What's gotten into you, old man? I mean, you're annoying at best, but I think your crazy comments were growing on me."

He peeked through his lids for a moment, and then returned to his meditation.

Fred sighed. It was going to be a lonely coma if Bill thought this was companionship. "Fine, keep quiet. You're missing out on the show."

Stan looked back at the body and sighed.

"Are you okay?" the nurse asked.

"I'm not dealing well with the grief of my father's passing. And worse, the one thing that could give me closure…" He touched the body's shoulder. "The department will not allow me to participate in my father's investigation any longer. I'm really not supposed to be here at all." He stared at the body, his face distressed. "All I want are answers."

Kari stepped forward and offered him a consoling grin. "I'm sorry. I know it is hard to lose somebody. I worry about that every day with my brother being in the Middle East. I can't imagine losing him. If you need to talk to someone not in a coma," she said with a soft grin, "I'm here. But if you want me to leave you alone, I get that, too."

"Thanks, Ms. Jensen. I appreciate that. Talking about it hasn't been easy."

"Kari, please." She smiled. "And I'm sure it hasn't. But they say talking is the best therapy."

"My name's Stan, but most of my friends call me Heller. Goes back to my military days, I guess. Calling everybody by his or her last names. Cops do it, too."

She sat on the stool. "So, you were in the service also?"

He looked around. "Is it okay that you're sitting in here with me? I mean, am I keeping you from doing rounds?"

Her eyes traveled to the clock on the wall. "I'm due a ten-minute break anyway."

Stan rolled his shoulders. "Yes, U.S. Army Intelligence for four years right out of high school. When I got out, I entered the police academy. Been with the San Diego department ever since."

"Was your dad a cop, too?"

"Yeah. He was a detective for thirty-plus years. Was about to get his gold watch, when..." His voice choked.

"You don't have to talk about it, if you don't want to."

"No, it's okay. Therapy right?"

She smiled.

He cleared his throat and continued, "My dad was assigned to investigate Mr. Avarice's shooting. It was the first of many to come, though he didn't know that at the time. At the second crime scene, something must have gone wrong, because he came out in a body bag."

"Wow."

In an obvious attempt to change the conversation, he waved in her direction. "What's your story?"

She stared at him a moment, then said, "I started college right away to become a nurse. I never deviated from that plan. I knew I wanted to help people. Having grown up only a mile from here, I even had this place in the back of my mind."

"That's impressive."

She smiled. "I suppose."

Stan looked back at the body. "Isn't it tough to care for coma patients?"

"I like it. They never complain about the work I do, and I get to do all the talking."

The two exchanged silent smiles.

"Yeah, they've got it bad." Fred glanced over at Bill. His eyes were now open and a funny smile played on his lips. "Aw, so you've come back to life. You have anything entertaining to say?"

He rolled his eyes and looked back at the couple. "I think it's time you return to the mirror. You obviously haven't learned a thing yet."

"Sure I have. I've learned how I got the big bucks."

Bill snapped his head toward Fred, his eyes ablaze. "You stole money from innocent people. Doesn't that bother you?"

Fred shrugged. "Not really. We robbed from the wealthy, not the poor. Think of us as Robin Hoods." He remembered the time his wife had mocked him by saying that and frowned.

Bill furrowed his brow. "And that makes it okay?"

"Sure. They probably got it just as dishonestly."

"As the Good Book says, 'God will bring to light what is hidden in darkness and will expose the motives of men's heart.'" The old man stood, glowered at him, and disappeared behind the curtain.

Fred stepped forward.

"Go to the mirror, Freddy," he yelled. "Go become a better man before you end up in a very dark place for an infinite amount of time."

Fred took one last look at Stan and Kari. They talked almost in a whisper, obviously enjoying each other's company. He stepped to the mirror. Was there a dark place such as hell? His aunt believed in such an ending. If she was right, he didn't want to go there. But how could he change if he didn't feel guilty about his past?

"To the mirror, big bucks," Bill yelled again.

Fred sighed and stared at the silver glass. Maybe he'd find some redeeming quality in remembering.

Chapter Seventeen

Stan ordered a large, black coffee and slid in a booth across from Kari. He didn't know why, but he felt at ease around her. She didn't push him to talk, but for some reason, he wanted to share with her.

"So, you really arrested that guy? Just for hitting you with a piece of gum?" She giggled a pleasant laugh, not like Melissa's annoying cackle.

"Yeah, you bet. I mean, he struck an officer. I had no choice."

"Don't you mean *stuck* an officer?" Her face lit up with amusement, and without a doubt, he liked her.

Sliding his cup to the side, he leaned in on both elbows, as if to reveal a secret. "Okay, out with it, Nurse Jensen. Tell me one stupid thing you've done on the job."

Her eyes darted side-to-side, then she matched his posture. "I…" She glanced around again for apparent dramatic effect, "…once ate a patient's pie."

He pinched his lips together, trying not to laugh. "I'm sorry, you did what?"

"It was chocolate cream, my favorite. You know…the kind with chocolate shavings and really good graham cracker crust." She bit the side of her cheek, in what seemed to be mock embarrassment. "Well… He had already slept through two meals, and I didn't want it go bad."

"So you ate it?"

"Yes." She laughed.

He couldn't help but join in her merriment. The best thing about being in her presence, for a few minutes, was the pain of losing his father dissipated in the recesses of his mind. His gaze fell to the dessert counter. He stood. "Give me a second." He felt her eyes on his back as he crossed to the ice-filled display case. "Can I get a piece of your chocolate cream pie, please?"

The woman handed it to him, and he handed her a five. "Keep the change."

Proudly, Stan returned to the table with his gift and placed it in front of her. "I thought, as a detective, I should keep you honest and on the straight and narrow. Here is your own pie."

Her entire face lit up.

"Well, aren't you going to eat it?"

She lifted a fork and pushed the pie to the center of the table. "Only if you join me."

"Deal." He grabbed a fork and slid it into the soft whipped cream-chocolate mixture and lifted it to his mouth. They chatted about nothing important, nothing all that interesting, but with her, he was not bored. Oh how he wished his dad could have met her.

After scraping the last crumb off the plate, she checked her watch. "Oh, it goes so fast."

"You have to go?"

"I'm afraid so." She stood and dropped her cup in a nearby trash can. "I had fun."

Me, too. "Maybe I'll see you around?"

"I hope so." She tucked a strand of hair behind her ear and stumbled back a few steps, then laughed. "Goodbye, Stan."

"Now that you've had your pie, try not to eat anybody's dessert tonight."

She laughed. "I'll try. But if it's chocolate, there are no guarantees."

He chuckled and then sighed as she waved and started for the corridor.

A cafeteria worker came behind him to clean the table. "You know, as depressing a place like this hospital is, I've never seen two people laugh so much."

Stan looked at the young lady and half-smiled, then started for the exit. She was right. It wasn't the happiest place on earth, but he couldn't help it. He really enjoyed his time here.

Chapter Eighteen

"Hello, Mrs. Jenkins," Lee said into the phone. "I'm glad you're home. I just got off the phone with my top agent and I have the most incredible news. Your investments have doubled in the last twenty-four hours."

A moment of silence and then the screaming began. "That's great. That's absolutely wonderful!"

"Yes it is. And I'm calling to tell you that with my help, you're going to be a very wealthy woman."

"Really?"

"Really. Just check your account." Lee swiveled around in his chair and looked out the large bay window that overlooked West B Street. "I know you were a little hesitant to invest your funds, but now you won't have to. I have a sure-fire ticket coming up. And anyone who jumps on board will walk away filthy rich. How does that sound?"

He loved this moment. The dramatic pause, and then the deep breathing.

Lee smiled. "You still with me, Mrs. Jenkins?"

"Yes, I'm still here."

Traffic below moved in a steady fashion. The city pumped like the beating of his heart. Never ending and full of adrenaline. "Good. Do you need to speak with your husband about this?"

She coughed. "Actually, I'm recently widowed. The

money I'm investing is my late husband's trust."

A car crashed into the fender of another car below. Time halted. Lee sat and closed his eyes. He'd been told Mrs. Jenkins was a woman snooping around the stock trade, eager to invest her money, yet anxious about doing so. She had the appearance of one with assets, but destitute enough to need more. The prime candidate. But not once had he considered this— swindling the money of an elderly widow. Was he growing a conscience? Without the money, she'd probably have nothing. He needed to know.

Lee loosened his tie and cleared his throat. "What sort of funds do you have outside his trust?"

"Well, I'm too old to work, and with social security not being what it used to be..." She took a deep breath. "Well, basically that's it. So, I'm glad to see I've been lucky in your capable hands."

Lee ran a hand through his hair several times. He didn't like this one bit. Was it too late to get out? He weighed the options. If he backed out, Melton and Gray would stand to lose the fifty thousand they invested in making her believe she was doing well. If he went through with it, she'd be left with nothing.

"Mr. Avarice? Are you still there?"

He squeezed his eyes closed for a moment. "Yes, I'm still here." He closed her file and stood. "I need to confer with my investors before I share the news with you. Will you be around tomorrow morning?"

"I have a doctor's appointment around eight, but I'll be home an hour or so after that."

"Fine. I'll call you then. Good-bye, Mrs. Jenkins."

"Good-bye."

The receiver buzzed in his ear. He set the phone

down and began to pace. He dreaded the call to Mr. Melton. His boss wasn't always an understanding man. Lee knew he couldn't take her money. That was at least clear. As much as he hated to admit it, he had a conscience. He was fine with extorting the jerks who invested their money poorly. But a widow? He had to pencil the line.

Wait. This isn't my fault. The recruiting department was supposed to do a thorough check on all clients before sending them on to me. Mrs. Jenkins's file should have never made it to my desk.

Someone knocked at the door.

"Yeah?" Lee said.

Candice peeked inside. "Mr. Melton is in the building."

A lump of fear lodged in Lee's throat. "Good. Make the arrangements for us to meet."

"Yes, sir." She shut the door.

This isn't good. Not good at all. *He could say it wasn't his fault all he wanted, but when the money hit the bank, it was his problem.*

The doorknob turned, and Mr. Melton entered. His tall, broad frame always made Lee shutter.

"Hello, Mr. Avarice. How are things going up here?"

Lee shook Melton's hand. "Good, sir. But I'm glad you stopped by today. I have a slight issue I'd like to discuss with you."

"Oh?" Melton raised an eyebrow.

"Yes, do you have the time?"

He placed his left hand around Lee's shoulder and squeezed. "For you. Always." He pushed Lee toward his desk and took a seat in an adjoining chair. "So, what can I do for you?"

"Well, a few weeks ago, I was given a file on an elderly lady named Tina Jenkins. She seemed like the perfect client for Melton and Gray. I didn't hold back. I worked her like everyone else and she bit." Lee swallowed. "And we doubled her money this morning."

Melton stared at him with a blank expression. "So, what's the problem?"

Lee twisted his lips and looked at the ceiling. "I just got off the phone with her, and it seems she's a recent widow." He met Melton's eyes again.

Melton blinked. He looked past Lee out the window, his mind a mystery. "You seem troubled by this news."

"Yes, sir. The money she invested was her late husband's trust. It's the only money she has to survive on. According to her file, she's in her early seventies. She's too old to get a job. Sir, please tell me there's something we can do to make this right."

Melton's eyes shot back to Lee's and narrowed. "Do? What do you expect us to do?"

Lee's tie seemed to suffocate him. He reached up and moved the knot side to side. "Can we give her the money back?"

A small, sardonic smile played across Melton's lips. "Who would have guessed? You have a conscience."

"I am human, sir."

Melton stood and placed both his hands on Lee's desk. "If we give her the money back, we have to give her the fifty thousand, too. You realize that?"

Lee shook his head. "Not if we say there was a clerical error. We could fudge somewhere."

Melton straightened and breathed in through his nose. "I think you're missing the bigger picture here."

"What's that?"

Melton's lips curled as he cornered the desk. "That I don't want you to have a conscience. You can't work for me if you have morals. This isn't a family company. You want to work for a feel good place? Then go work at an amusement park."

He reached for Lee's tie and pulled it tighter around his neck. "I brought you on, because I believed there was something about you that could do the job without looking back. You knew what we were about before I even offered you the position. This isn't Romper Room. You either do the task or get out." He released the tie, pushed on Lee's chair, and walked toward the door. "Finish her by the end of the week, or you're fired." Melton swung the door open and then slammed it behind him.

Lee's stomach lurched. He reached for the wastebasket, just in time to expel that morning's Danish and coffee. What am I doing here? *But he knew he had no choice. He grabbed a tissue from inside the drawer and blotted his mouth. Getting out would make him a certified witness to the biggest moneymaking scam on the west coast. They'd kill him before they'd let him walk.* Fire? *He was sure that was more literal in its meaning. He assumed it was implying the incinerator the mortician used for cremation or maybe the action of pulling a gun trigger. Either way, the word* fire *wasn't a good one.*

He then flipped open the folder on his desk and pointed to her phone number. He wouldn't wait until the next morning. He'd do it now. The sooner he got her file off his desk and in the vault, the sooner he could live with himself again.

****

Fred stared at his body on the table. The inert man's expression seemed so solemn. Peaceful. And yet, his mind, imagination, or soul—whatever he was now—was in turmoil.

"You don't look happy," Bill said from where he sat on the windowsill.

"Me or the stiff?"

"Aw, but you are one and the same. Are you not?"

Yeah, unfortunately. He sighed. "How did I get here, Bill? What awful thing did I do to end up in a coma?"

The old man laughed and leaned out the open window. "From what I've seen, I'd ask what did you do to deserve to live?"

Fred stood and pushed on Bill's shoulder.

The man wobbled and grabbed onto the side of the windowsill. "You cruel beast. You could have killed me."

Fred shook his head. "You're not flesh and blood. You'd be fine." He crossed and sat against the wall under the TV. Looking up, he said, "Why do they have a TV in here? I'm in a coma. It's not like I can watch it."

Bill pinched his fingers together, lifted them in the air, and closed his eyes. "The mystery just gets greater."

"And I'd like answers. Starting with that one."

Bill stuck his arm out the window and moved it through the air like one back floating in a pool of water. "You ever hear of Silas Lapham?"

Fred shook his head. "No, should I have?"

Bill shrugged. "You did go to school, did you not?"

"I took my GED and had my career established before my twentieth birthday. I never needed to."

"Explains a lot about you, Mr. Avarice."

"What's your point, old man?"

"In the nineteenth century, men and their money were on an up rise. Great wealth was obtained faster than any other time before that point." Bill mimicked picking up a fork and knife and cutting into food. "The rich were dining on lobster and caviar, living in plush high-rises, while everyone else suffered in the gutter. Famous author William Dean Howell wrote a book called *The Rise of Silas Lapham*."

"Nope, never heard of it."

"Yeah, well, in the story, he depicted the moral decay of one man to reach the top of the financial food chain."

"But he was successful, right?"

Bill jumped down and swung his arms at his sides. "No, he died a poor man. But he found solace in his journey."

Fred stretched out on the cold tile floor and yawned. "Poor men aren't happy. They're just delusional."

"That's where you're wrong. Do you know who John Jacob Astor was?"

"Yeah, multi-millionaire who owned a fur company." Fred smiled. "See, I'm not totally obtuse. I know where the money is. Or was."

Bill sat on the black stool. "Yeah, well, Astor said on his death bed that he was the most miserable man alive."

"So?" Fred shrugged. "One rich man was unhappy.

Big deal."

"John D. Rockefeller said, 'I have made millions, but they have brought me no happiness.'"

Fred pushed up on his elbows and faced Bill. "Look, it's too bad that all those guys had a bad time with their money. I'm not them. I wasn't a miserable tycoon. I had a great life. I ate where I wanted. I had an enormous suite at the top of a high-rise with my name on it. A house in Coronado. A beautiful wife."

Bill cleared his throat. "Had. *Had* a beautiful wife."

"I said money brought me happiness. Women aren't happiness, they're thorns in the side of mankind."

The old man let out a throaty chuckle. "They're from your rib, Mr. Cheerful. Besides, I can tell you weren't happy. Still aren't. I saw your last jaunt in the mirror. Did you end up stealing that widow's money?"

Fred shut his eyes. *Forget it*, he didn't want to think about his life anymore. Bill was right. There wasn't happiness here. But it had nothing to do with money. It had to do with breathing and existing in a life he hated. Not once since his dad left home had he felt joy. Nothing had ever been the same, and he still missed his mother. Peace was something he never experienced. Even in a coma, his mind couldn't rest. He had to fight through horrible memories and bad choices. He was forced to face who he really was in the mirror.

How much more can I endure? If he suddenly woke up from his coma, he would probably put a bullet in his head. He grabbed his head, kneeled forward, and touched his forehead to the floor. "This is hopeless. Go ahead and say it. My life is hopeless."

"You done with your pity party yet?" Bill leaned within an inch of his face.

Fred peeked to the side through his lids. "Would you mind backing off a bit? You're in my personal bubble."

"Don't mean to pop it." Bill smiled. "Just wondered what's stuffing that head of yours. You admitted it yet?"

He sat up. "Admitted what yet?"

"That you're unhappy."

"I'm unhappy with you sitting so close to me." Fred slid over an inch. Bill followed suit. Fred pushed again and Bill moved, too. Around the room. Push. Push. Push. Push. When they reached the bed, Bill blocked him in.

"What is your problem? Ever heard of personal space? Go away."

"But I like you."

Fred stood. "Well, I like you on the other side of the room. It's hard enough being confined in this space twenty-four seven without you breathing on me."

"Admit you're unhappy, and I'll give you that break."

Fred cocked his head to the side and crossed his arms. "Seriously? No tricks? You'll leave me alone."

"Scout's honor." Bill held up three fingers in the air and smiled. Fred opened his mouth to speak, but Bill cut him off. "Wait, I was never a scout. Maybe on my wife's grave."

"Fine."

"Nope, never had one of those either. Maybe I better just promise and leave the faith in your hands. Let my yes be yes and my no be no. This is a yes and it's yes."

"You finished?"

Bill winked.

"You're right. I'm not a happy person. But it isn't because of my money. It's because my life has stunk from infancy. Money at least gave me some sort of out." Fred sighed. "There now. You happy?"

A smile spread across Bill's face. "Ecstatic. Now don't you feel better?" He reached out to give Fred a hug.

"Peace, Bill. You promised me a break."

"So, I did. I'll see you later." And true to his word, Bill disappeared.

Chapter Nineteen

Stan sat in his squad car, writing a report on the crime he just investigated. His mind far from the case at hand, he kept blinking to focus. It had been a hard week. He'd spent the weekend cleaning out his dad's house, and every time he found something from his childhood, he transcended through each stage of grief. For obvious reasons, he lingered on anger.

To make matters worse, he'd received word that his sister was spotted again near the sunset pier with some goon. The fear of what she might be doing intensified each time his mind wandered. Ever since their mother died, she'd struggled to be good. She had pushed their dad to the limit daily, and following more than dozens of fights, eventually ran away. It didn't help that he'd treated her like less of a person after each illegal activity. Maybe if he'd tried to understand her, rather than judge her, she would have opened up and turned around.

He jumped at the tap on his window. It was Kari. After turning the key, he slid down the window. "Hi."

"Hi." She smiled.

"What are you doing here?"

"I live down the block. All my neighbors were out watching the excitement, so I joined them. I saw you in this car. I hope it's okay that I came over."

"Of course." He nodded. "Step back."

Kari returned to the sidewalk.

Stan exited the car and joined her. "Are you working tonight?"

"No, I just got off an hour ago. You?"

"I wasn't even supposed to be on today. But working keeps my mind off things, you know?" He glanced at his watch. "I'm probably due for a break. You want to grab a cup of coffee with me?"

"I'd love to. Can you give me a second to go change?" She opened her coat, revealing lavender scrubs.

"Absolutely. It'll give me a minute to finish up this report."

"Okay, be back in a flash." She waved and ran up the steps toward her apartment.

Stan got back into his car and stared at the yellow form in his hand. The letters seemed to dance on the page. *Great. Now I really can't concentrate.* He wrote his name on the top, check-marked a few places, and then wrote a short description of what happened. He signed his name and tossed it on the dashboard, just in time to see Kari walking toward his car.

Wow. She wore jeans and a rose-pink blouse. Her hair lay in soft waves around her shoulders and a silver cross hung around her neck. *Absolutely stunning.*

He jumped out and crossed to the passenger side. "You look nice," he said, opening the door.

"Thanks." She lowered her eyes and then ducked in the car. "Anything beats my uniform."

He closed the door and crossed back to his side. The clipboard still lay on the dashboard. He snatched it and tossed it in the backseat. "Any place you like to go?" He started the engine.

"I usually just drink the tar at the hospital. You choose."

He smiled. "It couldn't be any worse than the tar at the station. The cops brag about the hair it grows, and we chew it." He placed his arm on the back of her seat and pulled out into traffic. "I guess we can go to my place. It's just a block away."

Her eyes clouded.

"Oh, no." He laughed. "I meant my coffee place. Not my home."

The sound of relief escaped her lungs. "Sorry, I'm just..." She bit down on one of her fingernails. "Let's just say, I don't get out much. I'm sure you can tell."

"Yeah, well, me either." Stan maneuvered the car over to the curb and got out. He opened her door and together they crossed the street to *Just Brew It.*

"This is cute," she said as they stepped inside.

The walls were burgundy, covered with black and white stills of famous people drinking coffee, and studio lights illuminated the place. "It's owned by an eccentric woman who got lost in the sixties, but she has the best coffee in the city. What would you like?"

She studied the chalkboard covered in choices. "The German chocolate mocha sounds heavenly."

"You like coconut?"

"Love it." She smiled.

He returned her smile. "A girl after my own heart." He turned to face the owner and tried not to internally judge the barista's feathered muumuu and polka-dot beret.

"Ah, Stanley, so good to see you're out with such a pretty girl."

"Thanks," Kari said, a touch of pink in her cheeks.

"You want your usual?" She grabbed for a plastic cup.

"No, I think I'll join the lady tonight. We'll take two large German chocolate mochas."

Kari cupped her hand over his ear and whispered, "Decaf."

"One decaf." He turned back to Kari. "You want a pastry?"

"I'm not that hungry."

Beatrice shook her head. "You've got to have a pastry, even if you're not hungry. They're the best."

"She's right. I'll have one brownie-nut scone warmed with whip cream and two forks."

"You're relentless," Kari said.

He winked. "One bite and you'll change your mind."

"It's chocolate. I already have."

He laughed.

Beatrice handed them their order, and Stan handed her the money. "See you tomorrow."

"You want your receipt?"

He shook his head and nodded for Kari to follow. "Where would you like to sit?"

His date pointed to a couple of overstuffed chairs in the far left corner.

"Great choice. Now run before someone else grabs them."

She laughed and took off for the chairs. A gothic-looking girl almost sat down, but Kari beat her to it. The girl rolled her eyes and walked away. Kari sat, giggling, with her coffee pressed firmly against her chest.

Stan joined her, laughing. "That was great. I can

tell you're a woman who gets what she wants."

She took a sip and settled back into the chair. "I wouldn't say that."

He placed the scone on a little coffee table between them and handed her a fork. "Why not?"

She shrugged. "I don't go after much, so I don't have much."

"You have an education and a job you love." He pushed his plastic fork into the flaky dough and lifted it to his mouth. The crumbly chocolate practically melted on his tongue. He swallowed. "That's more than some."

"Yes, but it isn't a big deal. I spend all my waking hours either at work or at home." She reached down and grabbed a small crumb from the plate. She examined it and then popped it in her mouth. "Wow, that is good."

"Told you." He sipped his coffee, watching her over the rim of the cup. Her beautiful eyes danced with life. It had been a long time since he had wanted to be around a woman. But she was special. This he knew. "What do you *want* to do?"

She shrugged.

"No, really. If you could do anything you wanted, starting today, what would it be?"

"I'd go on a cruise down the Mexican Riviera. Then I'd take another cruise in the Bahamas. And if I wasn't too sea sick, I'd take an Alaskan cruise." She smiled and stabbed a piece of the flaky pastry.

"Then why don't you?"

She sighed. "Fear maybe. Comfort, money, who knows? I've been alone so long that it's easier to just do what I know to do, rather than what I want to do."

"Don't you have family? I mean, besides your

brother?"

She shook her head. "No. It's just him and me. Has been for some time. If he died, I'd be alone in this world. Well, me and God."

He smiled. "I know what that's like."

"I'm sorry, I didn't mean..." She squeezed her lips together.

"Don't apologize. It's fine. Look, I'll admit, this is unusual for me. I haven't been out with anyone in a long while. I don't socialize anymore." He sighed. "With anyone. I guess I'm afraid if I have a good time, I'm forgetting about my dad. Is that stupid?"

She placed her hand on his, sending a shiver up his arm.

"I don't think it's stupid. It makes a lot of sense. I see that a lot in my job. People come to my hospital to die. Grief is a natural process. Everyone has a different way of grieving, and no one should criticize it."

"Very profound." He toasted with his coffee in the air. "How'd we get so serious?"

"I don't know, but I'm having a good time."

"Me, too."

They finished their coffee and walked back to the car. He opened her door, and she moved to climb in. Their eyes locked. His heart pumped like mad in his chest. He couldn't help it; he wanted to kiss her. He leaned forward, his gaze roving from her eyes to her mouth, and then his dad raced through his memory. He jerked back and dropped his head.

Kari climbed in the car slowly and he slammed the door behind her, not missing her look of disappointment.

What is wrong with me?

109

Chapter Twenty

"You going in again?" Bill asked.

Fred looked over his shoulder at the quirky man and smiled. Despite the long robe he wore, his wrinkled arms and legs were almost always exposed. "Yeah, I suppose I will."

"Good luck. You're going to need it."

"Thanks for the encouragement, old man. You're always good for that."

"Coma companion at your service." He snapped to attention and saluted.

"You're kind of crazy. You know that?"

Bill beamed. "Your crazy coma companion comes constantly `cause coma corpses can't corner compassion."

"Okay, I'd like to buy a rephrase for a thousand. You're psychotic."

"One man's wisdom is another man's crazy."

Shaking his head, Fred turned to the mirror and stared hard. He wanted answers; he just hated the truth—that they could only be found from within.

****

Lee stepped out of the limo and onto the red carpet. Flashes of light and chaotic screaming sliced through the night. Ahead of him, he could see the back of his newest client. Beth Snow. She was a new movie producer in Los Angeles seeking quick collateral to fund her next project. Striking, with her shoulder-length black hair and violet-blue eyes, no one let her appearance deceive them for long. A power-hungry woman, used to controlling those around her, she was an icon among many females in the business world. Lee salivated over the possibility of bringing her down. From the day they met, her harsh words and demeaning attitude sliced his ego. He hungered for the day he would deliver the bad news about her empty bank account. He pressed rewind on his cognitive VCR and played it in his mind for the millionth time. I'm sorry, Beth. I don't know what happened, but the stocks plummeted and you're dead broke. *With a mental pat on his back, he tugged at his tux jacket, smiled to himself, and strolled into the main hall.*

"Aw, Lee Avarice, welcome," she said, extending her hand bent at the wrist. "Your boss allowed you to get away."

He took her fingers in his and grinned. "Ms. Snow, I am my boss, and thanks for inviting me."

"Ah, Beth will do. Come, there's someone I'd like you to meet." She waved for him to follow her.

Lee stepped past the final rope and into the golden ballroom. Orchestra music filtered through the air, waiters flowed by with trays of champagne, and rainbows danced off the diamond-decorated necks in the room. Ahead of him stood a short Asian man, with thick glasses and an Armani suit. He didn't smile, but offered his hand.

"Ping Chow, this is my investment advisor, Lee Avarice. Avarice, meet Mr. Chow." She eyed Lee. "My lawyer."

Lee gulped and forced a smile. "Nice to meet you. I

guess together we're taking good care of the next big Hollywood producer."

"Let's hope so. For your sake, Mr. Avarice." Mr. Chow bobbed his head once and left for the buffet line.

Lee forced a taut grin in Beth's direction and then peered around the room. "Well, if you'll excuse me, there's someone I need to see."

Of course, Lee didn't know anyone else at the party. This was Beth's event. Not his. All of a sudden, he felt off-balance. Did she suspect something? How could she? She hadn't invested yet. At this point, she'd merely shown interest. Maybe he should walk away. Wait. What am I saying? I'll never get this good a gig again. *She was worth more than all his clients combined.* It is just cold feet. *Besides, he would enjoy the kill.*

He went to the washroom. A well-dressed gentleman waited on a stool just inside the door. Lee went to the counter, and the attendant handed him a towel. "Thank you."

"Certainly, sir."

Lee splashed a handful of water on his cheeks, then dabbed the cloth against his face. He had to get control. Beth was a tough woman. Any regress on his part could end in disaster ten feet under. Lee dug in his pocket, pulled out a five, and popped it in the tin on the counter. The attendant nodded and Lee walked back to the floor.

"Excuse me," *a woman said behind him.*

He turned around. Beth.

"Did you find who were you looking for?" *The smirk on her face implied her suspicion.*

What? Who was I...? *"Oh, no. I didn't."*

"Maybe I could help?" Her eyes appeared almost violet in the light, beautiful in combination with her fair skin.

Stop. She's not beautiful. She's the enemy. An enemy who would eat me alive if I hand her the fork. *The orchestra began to play a soft waltz. He had to change the subject. "Would you like to dance?"*

"Sure. I'd love to." She put out her hand and stepped into his arms. They glided around the ballroom floor in a fluid motion. She leaned into his ear and the smell of perfume and brandy wafted to his nose.

"I know what you're up to, Mr. Avarice," she whispered, her breath tickling the hairs on his neck. *"And you and I, we'll stop this little charade and be candid."* She pulled back and met his gaze. *"I like people who work with me to be honest."*

His heart thundered in his chest; his palms clammy.

"I know you're a fraud, but lucky for you, I don't plan to expose you. Rather, I'd like you to do me a favor instead."

"What's that?" His voice squeaked. He cleared his throat. Get a grip.

Her gaze fell to the sea of people dancing next to them and then drew him close. "I want you to pretend to love my daughter."

He pushed away. "What?"

She positioned her arms around his neck and pulled him tight. "Act natural and listen to me. My daughter is only five years younger than you. I may look young, but don't let a little plastic surgery fool you." She lifted a piece of lint from his collar and tossed it aside. *"Now listen, she's involved in something I can't condone and it will take the right man to bring her around. You don't have to marry her, just sway her to sanity. I assume you have no religious affiliations?"*

"What? No. But why me?"

"Because you're a con man, Mr. Avarice. And from what I've seen, a really good one."

His eyes met hers. "And yet, I didn't fool you."

She smiled. "No, Mr. Avarice. You did." She glanced at the diminutive man stuffing his face in the corner. "Mr. Chow is also Gray's lawyer."

"What?"

Her lips curled into an impious grin. "Next time you might consider cross-checking who does business with whom."

Lee dropped his gaze. He felt as if he was spinning on a carousel—he wanted off. "So, what is it that your daughter's into?"

Her lips tightened. "God."

****

Lee peered in his bathroom mirror and turned his chin side to side. Handsome as always. *He winked then poured a handful of aftershave in his hands. He rubbed them together and then slapped them against his face. He winced at the sting, but then relaxed as it cooled, soothing his skin.*

He walked into his bedroom and looked at the suit leaning against the Oriental black headboard. His hands trembled. He rubbed them together. Why was he so nervous? He climbed into his outfit and grabbed a few ties from the closet. He held them up in the mirror, one at a time. It was a simple choice. Red or blue?

He stepped down into the sunken living room

where his business partner, Don Crary, sat cross-legged on the black leather couch, cracking peanuts, watching a basketball game. His friend glanced up. "So when do you pick her up?"

"Don't spill shells on my sofa cushions."

"Answer the question."

"Half an hour." Lee held a blue tie in his left hand and a red tie in his right. "Which one?"

Don looked from one tie to the other. "Is that the suit you're wearing?"

Lee looked down at his blue pinstripe. "Yeah."

"Neither. You need something more hip. You got silver?"

Lee wrinkled his nose. "I'm not wearing one of those skinny rocker ties you wear. Red or blue?"

"You said this girl is young. She's going to expect you to leave the grandpa ties from the seventies in your closet. It's the eighties...get with it, dude."

Lee threw back his head and mouthed, "Why me?"

"Because, you're a con man. And with every job, there are perks and there are draw backs."

"These are the drawbacks," they said together and then laughed.

"Red," Don said.

"Thank you." Lee whipped the tie under his collar and around to the front, then moved to the big bay windows overlooking the ocean. He pulled up the blinds, letting in the afternoon sun.

"So, what's the deal with this chick anyway? You were very vague with me over the phone." Don pinched the shell of a nut open in his hand and picked out the pieces.

"Beth gave me her daughter's likes and dislikes.

115

She told me where she'll be and what to do." Lee spotted an empty nut shell on his white rug and glared at Don. "Don't mess up my house."

"What?" His friend tried to play innocent.

Lee shook his head and tossed the shell on the top of the bar.

"What are your plans for tonight?"

"Tonight she's at a concert in downtown, and I have a ticket within feet of her."

"Who's playing? Bon Jovi? Billy Idol? I heard Madonna is coming to town. I'm so jealous if it's Madonna."

"The La Nuit Chamber Singers." Lee smiled. "Still jealous?"

Don laughed. "No."

Lee walked back to his room and grabbed a pair of argyle socks out of his top drawer and penny loafers from the closet. He sat down on the chair by the couch and pulled them on. "I guess she's into all sorts of artsy stuff. Her mom said she's an art major at SDSU."

"A college girl, huh? Yeah, that'll happen." Don snickered and popped a nut in his mouth. He gagged, his face red. Coughing, he dislodged the piece into his hand.

Lee smiled. "Karma, man."

Don tossed the nut onto the table and rubbed his watery eyes. "I didn't think you believed in reincarnation."

"I don't. I believe in what comes around goes around. You badmouth me, you just might choke on a peanut. Karma."

Don shook his head. "As you were saying."

"Anyway, I have her schedule. Tomorrow she'll be

at an art exhibit in Old Town, and Wednesday, she's to attend a cultural festival at Balboa Park."

"If she's the Bohemian you've described her to be, are you sure she'll stick to the plan?"

Lee shrugged. "Her mom was pretty certain she'd be at all of those places."

Don scooted forward and brushed shells from his pants onto the glass table. "So, what do you plan to do? Stalk her?"

"Sort of. But tastefully." Lee grabbed his wallet from the kitchen counter. "After running into her a few times, I'm sure to get her number."

"If it was me, it wouldn't take but a second."

"Yeah, I'm sure. But this is a long con. In the end, it must appear to be her idea." Lee grabbed his jacket and pulled it on. "I need to make her trust me. It won't be enough to make a difference if it's just a fling. She has to love me enough to desert her faith."

Don smirked. "What is she? Hari Krishna or something?"

"Catholic or Christian. Not sure."

Don raised his left eyebrow. "And that's bad, because why?"

"Look, I think whatever she wants to believe is her business. I'm not out to judge this girl. It's just a job that pays well. Plain and simple."

"Aren't you afraid you'll get struck by lightning or something. You don't even know why you're doing it?"

"Clean up your mess," Lee said staring at the shell-covered glass. "From what I can figure out, her mom wants to be a big shot in Hollywood. Most of the big players are either Jewish or into Scientology. There's a real bad taste toward whatever she is into,

and I guess her daughter is very boisterous about her faith."

His friend flipped over the back of the couch and grabbed his coat from the stool at the bar. "Still doesn't explain why you're involved."

"She has a weakness for hot guys." Lee winked, snatched up his keys from the counter, and tucked them in his jacket pocket.

"And I guess you're a hot guy?"

"What can I say?"

"Oh brother."

"It's simple. Every stupid decision the girl has ever made has happened because of a guy. And every time she's had a relationship turn sour, she goes running to her mom for comfort and advice. Beth is banking on that."

"That she'll leave all her beliefs behind for you?"

Lee opened the door and waved his friend through. "What girl wouldn't?"

Dan slipped past him. "I can think of about a million."

"The gift of any con man is knowing what the other person wants to hear. It's called charm. And charm I've got." He shut the door and locked it. "You'll see. Two weeks. Her only reason for going to church again will be to marry me."

"You're going to marry her?"

His heart skipped. "Of course not. You know I'm not the marrying type." He walked to his car with Don in tow. "I said she'd want to marry me."

"You want to put your money where that hole is in your face?"

Lee reached into his pants and slapped a wad of

hundred dollar bills on the hood of his car. "Two weeks."

"You're on."

Chapter Twenty-One

Lee reached in his jacket pocket and pulled out the diamond bracelet Beth gave him the night before. It had been a gift from the late Mr. Snow to his daughter years ago. The token would be Lee's keycard to conversation. His palm tightened around the dainty jewelry, waiting for his moment of opportunity.

The gorgeous Elena Snow sat one seat away. Her dark hair, porcelain skin, and blue eyes made him imagine what her mother must have looked like years before plastic surgery was needed. The woman's smile lit up in the dark theatre, and he knew acting interested would come naturally. It was almost a crime to take the mother's money.

The orchestra finished a number and he reached over the empty seat and tapped her arm. "Excuse me."

She glanced at him, her eyes bright and full of life. "Yes?"

"Did you drop this?" The diamonds resting in his open palm danced in the dim light.

Quickly, she snatched it up, smile gone. "Where'd you get this?"

He pointed by her foot. "I noticed it when I moved into my seat."

"I didn't wear it tonight." Confusion clearly rested on her face as she studied the bracelet, probably confirming it was hers.

"Are you sure it's yours?" He stuck out his hand as if to take it back.

"Yeah, I'm sure." She closed her hand around it. *"I just don't know how it got here."*

Below, the conductor tapped his stand and the musicians readied themselves for another number. *"Maybe it was in your purse or coat,"* Lee whispered and then faced the stage with intent. Though he sensed her eyes still on him, he pretended to be interested in what lay on the stage. Their encounter had to be her idea. In his peripheral view, the outline of her mouth was slightly open as if she wished to say something. A second or two went by, and her gaze returned forward.

The concert played out beautifully. Lee had taught himself to be cultured. In his line of work, it helped to know all sorts of the humanities. Though at first he found staring at paintings and listening to music a bore, he had eventually trained himself to like it.

The house lights turned on.

Lee stood, grabbed his coat, and turned for the aisle away from Elena.

"Sir?"

He closed his eyes for a second and smiled. Yes! Slowly, he turned to face her.

"I just wanted to thank you. An expensive trinket like this could easily find its way into a pawn shop."

He nodded but didn't smile. *"You're welcome. But for the record, I'm not one to steal."*

"That's obvious."

"Did you enjoy the concert?"

"Yes, but I prefer the theater." Her gaze fell to the stage for a moment, and then back to him. *"Have you ever been?"*

"To a play?" He leaned against the seat in front of him and crossed his ankles. "I've been to Shakespeare at the Old Globe once. I couldn't understand everything, but it was good, I suppose."

"Good?" She brought her hands to her chest. "It was likely better than good." Her eyes widened. "I'd love to see Shakespeare at the Old Globe. I've seen several shows on Broadway, but never Shakespeare. I adore him. What show did you see?"

The information and their conversation read almost like a script. Lee was prepared for this with her favorite. "I saw Macbeth."

"No, way! I'm so jealous. That's my all-time favorite play." She clasped her hands together and said in a thick British accent, "Double, double, toil and trouble. Fire burn, and cauldron bubble."

Lee lifted his eyebrows and glanced around the room. Luckily, most of the people had already filtered into the lobby. "Well, I should probably go. It was nice meeting you."

"Elena. Elena Snow." She put out her hand.

He took it and held it. "Lee Avarice."

"Nice to meet you, Lee. Are you a coffee drinker? Would you like to join me for a cup a short way from here?"

He almost laughed. Beth said her daughter was a sucker for guys, but he expected a few more encounters to get a date. "Yes, I love coffee. And sure."

She looped her arm through his, and together, they walked out of the theatre and down the block. The sidewalk was packed with people, laughing, talking, and moving from one bar to another. Lee weeded though the crowd, checking ever so often to make sure

Elena wasn't far behind. Even through the spirited city, he spotted what must have been the place—a brown sign with gold painted letters Where You Bean?.

"Do you always have coffee with strange men?" he asked, once they were seated at a small table in the corner.

She laughed. "Well, I've already established you're not a crook, you love Shakespeare, you enjoy classical music, and you have a nice smile." She took a sip of her caramel mocha, watching him over the rim.

"And that's enough?"

"Oh, and your name is Lee Avarice. So, in my book, you're no longer a stranger."

"You're quite a unique girl, Ms. Snow." Surprisingly, he meant it.

"Unique. Yeah, that's a good definition for me. I'm very eclectic in my tastes. I love art, literature, music, theatre, as you probably already deduced. But I'm also into Ferris wheels, junk food, and punk-rock music. I don't cuss, smoke, or do drugs. I never shut up. And I don't get spooked." She leaned in. "But I'm religious."

"You in a nutshell?"

"Yep. Me in a nutshell. Though I'm allergic to peanuts."

"Well, I like what I see." Weird. No con. He meant it. They had a connection, which intrigued him.

"And how about you, Mr. Avarice?"

"Lee, please." He took a sip of his coffee.

"Okay, Lee. Tell me about you in a nutshell."

He sighed. The memorized speech he'd prepared seemed stupid now. He didn't want to con her, but rather to tell her the truth. "Me in a nutshell? I'm not that complicated. I'm a businessman who loves classical music. On occasion, I'll go to the theatre or to an art museum, but that isn't who I am." There. That was the truth with still an ounce of bait.

"You like art?"

He grabbed a napkin from the table and nodded. "Yeah, I suppose I do."

"Well, I'm going to an art exhibit in Old Town tomorrow. I know this may be a bit forward since I just met you, but would you want to go with me?"

He smiled. "Somehow I would never see that as too forward for you. You seem to live your life on an edge that most stand back from."

A small dimple marked her cheek as she grinned. "You've figured that out already?"

He winked. "When shall I pick you up?"

****

"Is it just me, or are they acting weird?" Bill said from behind him.

Fred blinked and faced his coma companion. The old man stood next to where Stan and Kari were visiting next to Fred's body. Both of them were eating sandwiches, chips, and soda, laughing.

"So, that was it?" Stan popped a chip in his mouth. "That's all you had to do?"

Nodding, Kari dabbed her mouth with a napkin. "That was it."

"What are they talking about?" Fred said.

Bill sat on the floor inches from Stan's leg. "She told some story about a promotion she got from pretending to make a coma patient talk."

"What?"

"You had to have been there." Chuckling, Bill wiped his eyes. "It was quite the story."

"I guess." Fred sat with his back against the wall. "Speaking of stories, did you happen to catch mine?"

The old man peered up through his lids. "You weren't right to trick that poor girl."

Fred laughed. "Don't judge me until you see how it plays out."

"You aren't a nice man, Freddy." Bill hopped up on his feet and circled the body. "And I think that unless you figure out real quick how to redeem yourself, you're going to have a very dark future awaiting you."

Fred pulled his legs to his chest and rested his chin on his knees. "I just want to get back to my life."

Bill shook his head. "You're hopeless."

"Maybe I am."

He walked back to Fred and sat on the floor next to him. He pulled his legs to his chest, mimicking Fred's posture.

"Go away."

"No. I have a question for you."

Fred let out exasperated breath. "What's that?"

"You said she was religious gal?"

"So *she* said."

"And she didn't convince you to be of the same faith?"

"She had no life plan. In the time I knew her, she claimed to be Christian, Buddhist, Greek Orthodox, Zen, and Unitarian."

Bill frowned. "So, then her mom was worried for all the wrong reasons."

"Look, all I know is Beth understood her daughter needed a distraction." Fred ran a hand over his head. "I offered her that."

"But I bet Ms. Snow never banked on you two falling in love."

His stomach flipped as if it was yesterday. "No, you're right there. She didn't."

Chapter Twenty-Two

"You really like this place?" Elena glanced around the Museum of Modern Art. *"I mean, I love it, but you?"*

"Why not me?" Lee kissed each of her knuckles one at a time.

She withdrew her hand. *"Because from the moment I met you six months ago, I knew you weren't a foo-foo kind of guy."*

"Foo-foo? What's that?"

She twirled around the room, her long skirt sweeping the floor. *"You know. Artsy stuff. Soft science. Not hard science. The lack of logic. Subjective, not objective."*

He grabbed her around the waist and swayed. *"You mean everything you're about?"*

"Exactly." She kissed the end of his nose.

"Well, that's just ridiculous, because I love you and you're a foo-foo kind of girl. So, I'm okay with being a foo-foo kind of guy."

"Hmmm?" She eyed him playfully with fake disbelief.

"Why do you go out with a dud like me?"

She drew close and whispered, her hot breath sending chills up his spine, *"Because I like the fact we're complete opposites. It's more balanced that way."*

Lee reached into his pant pocket and toyed with the small box. His heart hammered in his chest. The woman he had fallen for never looked so beautiful. Her hair was swept back from her face; a few dark brown ringlets caressed her neck. Now was the time.

"Are you okay?" she asked, a concerned look in her eyes.

"There is one piece of art in this place I know you haven't seen yet. And I think it expresses my love for you better than anything else in here."

Her eyes darted around the room at the warped metal, dismembered clay limbs, and slaps of paint on canvas. "Which one?"

Lee kneeled on one knee and held out the black box cupped in both hands. "This one."

A smile lit in her eyes as she slowly scooped it up. Like a child, she peeked inside. A solitaire-diamond ring set in platinum rested on white satin. "It's gorgeous."

"So are you."

She met his gaze. "Is there a question to go with this ring?"

"Of course." He took her hand in his. "Elena Snow, I love you more than I ever thought was possible. Will you spend the rest of your life with me as my wife?"

She pulled him up by the collar and plastered him with kisses, squeezing him tight. "Yes. Yes. Yes!"

"Is that a yes?"

"Absolutely yes!" She laid her head against his shoulder, and together, they walked to a bench in the corner of the room. He placed the ring on her finger and she held it out in front of her. "My mom is going to

love you."

Lee diverted his eyes. He had to tell her, but the woman he loved beamed with joy and he hated to ruin it. She's happy, but I have to tell her. *"About that…"*

Instant worry clouded her eyes as she faced him.

"It's no coincidence that I sat next to you on the night of the concert."

She raised an eyebrow. "Really?"

"Your mother gave me the ticket."

She lowered her hand into her lap. "Did she pay you?" Her voice flat, distant.

Lee pivoted his body to face her. "No. It wasn't like that."

"Did she give you the bracelet?" Her expression was cold, steeled. This was obviously not the first time she had asked this sort of question.

He put his head down and nodded. "Yeah."

She didn't speak for a moment, a minute that seemed like an hour. He watched her, searching. Finally, she said, "I know."

"What?"

Like the sun at dawn, a smile broke across her features. "I've known all along, but I needed you tell me the truth."

"You knew all along?"

In a mocking male voice, she said, "Maybe it was in your purse or jacket." She laughed. "Come on. How stupid did you think I was? I keep that chain locked up. The whole thing had dear old Mom written all over it."

"And yet you still dated me? Why?"

"Because my mother has great taste in men. Every guy she's ever set me up with has been great. I figured she'd only send the best." She licked her lips and

added, "And I couldn't resist finding out."
"And you still want to marry me?"
Her eyes waltzed with delight. "Without a doubt."

****

The precinct was almost devoid of human activity. Most of the officers were sent home to enjoy Christmas Eve with their family. Stan didn't have one, so there he sat, twirling a silver pen in circles on his desk. The phone hadn't made a sound in hours, and the streets seemed serene. It wasn't customary for crime to go down this time of year. It was more apt to go up, but something about this evening was different.

He let out a deep sigh and glanced around the dark, empty room. His eyes stopped at Kessler's desk in the corner. The desk lamp was on, spotlighting a red file on the lower left side.

Stan twirled the pen again but kept his eye on the folder. It had to be the tycoon murders. No case had been that big in a while. He tossed the pen in his drawer and debated his next move. He reached into his pocket and withdrew a stick of gum. He unfolded the foil wrapper while keeping his eye on the file. *That's it.* He rolled back and stood. His stomach flipped. He sat again. He imagined a fluorescent arrow flashing above Kessler's desk blinking, "Open, open, open." He looked over both shoulders and rose again. Another quick glance around the room confirmed he was alone. Cracking his knuckles, he stepped forward.

A door slammed in the hallway, and he tripped, almost choking on his gum. He steadied himself and then remained still, listening. The only thing audible seemed to be his labored breathing. *All clear.* He looked around the room again and then walked toward the prize. His heart pounded in his chest. He was a detective and knew how to scope out a suspect. He walked past the desk and peeked over his shoulder. The case number was in plain sight. He twisted around and looked. Yes, it was the one.

With one final glance around the room, he flipped the folder open. His father's coroner picture sat on top, blood seeping from an open hole in his temple. Stan swallowed against the bile in his throat. He reached for the trashcan. No, he was okay. He could do this. He wiped his brow and set the pile of pictures aside. The pages underneath listed all the evidence they'd collected so far. Stan scanned through each page at a maddening pace. Names, dates, places, and situations all listed in black and white. He consumed every nugget like a man who hadn't eaten in months.

Suddenly, a light switched on in the captain's office. Stan shuffled all the papers back in place and stuffed the pictures back on top. He closed the cover and bent down to tie his shoe just as the captain walked through the door. *Oh no, loafers.* He was wearing loafers. *What now?*

"Heller? Is that you down there?"

He spotted a dime, stood, and smiled. "Yes, captain. Just grabbing a dropped dime." He held up his shiny prize between his thumb and index finger.

"I see." The captain came around the desk and looked down at Stan. "What are you still doing here?"

"Someone had to stay behind. Everyone else had family dinners to get to."

The captain offered a consoling smile. "Yes, well, I'm here now. Why don't you take off?"

Stan crossed to his desk and seized an open water

bottle. "I'm fine, sir. You should go home to your family. I'm sure they miss you."

The captain shook his head. "No, my kids are all in bed, and this is the best duty time for me. I want you to go out and enjoy yourself. That's an order."

The recollection of the pages Stan just read filtered through his mind. *Why am I fighting this?* It was the perfect opportunity for him to digest all he'd just seen. Maybe do a little reconnaissance work. "Okay, Cap. I'll go."

The portly man raised an eyebrow. "Really?"

Stan nodded. "Really." He grabbed his jacket from the back of his chair and moved toward the entrance. "Good night, sir."

"Merry Christmas, Heller."

"Same to you, sir."

He pushed through the glass doors and ran to his Jeep. The air was brisk, but the sky seemed clear. He unlocked his door and jumped in. A feeling he hadn't known in months washed over him. Hope.

Chapter Twenty-Three

Stan started the engine and pulled out onto the desolate street. Inside his coat pocket, his cell phone rang. He reached for it and flipped it open. "Hello?"

"Merry Christmas, Stan," Kari said.

"Well, hello." He stopped at the light and repositioned the phone to his left hand. "Merry Christmas."

"I hope I'm not disturbing you."

He shook his head and drove through the green light. "No, not at all. What's up? Is Mr. Avarice awake?"

"No, nothing like that. I just wondered what you were doing for dinner tomorrow evening." She cleared her throat. "I just thought that since you and I are both without a family, I could make a ham dinner for us."

Stan worked to clear his mind. He didn't want to be distracted. Rather, he'd prefer to find his father's killer. But he liked Kari and didn't want to chase her off, the way he had Melissa. Besides, it was Christmas. He should go eat ham. "Okay, what time?"

"How about five?"

The light in front of him turned red and he stopped at the white line. "Five it is. Should I bring anything?"

She grinned. "Yourself."

He nodded and returned her smile. "Good night, Kari."

"Good night." She paused. "And Stan?"

"Yes?"

"I hope this wasn't too forward of me."

"No, not at all. I'll see you tomorrow. Night." For a moment, he sat at the green light. The wet roads swished as an occasional car flew past. His house was less than a block away. The light turned red. He placed his phone back in his jacket and waited, his mind on a million things. The light turned green. This time he went. In moments, he was down the long street and into his driveway. Shutting off the engine, he let himself think about Kari. He liked her, but the heavy feeling of grief might possibly get in the way. How could he ignore the information he'd just been given for a ham dinner?

Stan could hear the conversation as if his father was in the car.

You've got to eat, son. And with a pretty lady, no less. Have I taught you nothing?

Yes, Dad, but I need to concentrate on your killer first. Tomorrow is the perfect day to work on your case.

How am I ever going to get grandchildren if you keep pushing all the good ones away?

Yes, Dad. But the guilt of having fun without you hurts. "Don't be stupid, son."

His dad probably would have liked Kari but might have said she was too sweet for him. He sniffed and ran a hand through his hair. Time to stop thinking of what could have been and break this case—to find closure and justice. The one-story brown house in front of him mocked him. It represented a lifetime of holidays with his old man. With reluctance, he climbed out of the car and went inside. The room lay bare of any evidence it was Christmas. *Stop feeling sorry for yourself and get cracking.*

He tossed his jacket on the couch, his rumbling stomach urging him to the kitchen. At this point, he could eat anything. The opening of the refrigerator greeted him with the smell of something rotten. He let the door close and checked the cabinets instead. Not much more there. It looked like it was either frozen Salisbury steak or canned ravioli. Ravioli was quicker. He grabbed the can, pulled the ring on the top, dumped it in a plastic bowl, and popped it in the microwave. A minute and half later he was eating preservative-filled Italian cuisine, chased by root beer.

Once he'd eaten enough to think, he reached in his desk drawer and snatched a notepad and pen. It would take an all-nighter to remember everything from the file, but that was okay. He wouldn't be able to sleep anyway.

****

Lee glanced at the faceplate of his cell phone. Snow Enterprises. Here we go. *"Hello, Beth," he said with confidence.*

"I was calling to give you some good news."

Sliding into a booth at the Corner Deli, he flipped open a menu with his free hand. "What's that?"

The waitress set a glass of water in front of him and he motioned for her to give him a moment. She nodded and walked away.

"You're no longer in my debt," Beth said. "I'm releasing you of your obligation."

"I'm not sure what you're saying."

She laughed. "I'm saying you're free, Mr. Avarice. You no longer have to date my daughter."

His stomach swayed. How did he respond?

"*You're speechless. Well, I know it wasn't fair of me to ask you to do that in the first place, but I do thank you.*"

"*You're welcome.*" *He couldn't breathe.* "*Look, Ms. Snow...*"

"*Beth.*"

"*Beth. What if I didn't want to stop dating your daughter?*"

There was a moment of silence and then she laughed. "*She got to you, too, did she?*"

"*To me too?*" *The waitress started coming and he waved her off again.* "*What do you mean?*"

"*It happens every time I set her up with someone. They fall for her, but as soon as I tell her it was my idea, she's out of their life. You won't be any different. I assure you.*"

This woman was worse than he thought. How despicable. Of course, he agreed, didn't he? But he loved her. Really loved her. Beth didn't care about her daughter, as much as she cared about her own precious reputation and fulfilling her need to be loved. "*She already knows about our arrangement.*" *He took a deep breath.* "*And we're engaged.*"

"*Excuse me?*" *Beth said.*

He switched the phone from one ear to the other. "*I asked her last weekend, and she accepted.*"

"*We shall see.*" *The line fell silent.*

The waitress returned, poised and raring to go. "*Are you ready to order, sir?*"

Lee stared at the menu. The words seemed to blur together. "*Just bring me a coffee and bagel for now.*"

She snatched his menu and walked away, obviously

unhappy for the tip she'd received on a seventy-five-cent coffee and dollar bagel. Join the club, lady. It's not my day either.

****

Melton stormed into the room and slammed his hand down on Lee's desk. "What were you thinking?"

Lee looked up from the charts in his hands. "I'm sorry?"

"You're going to be." His boss sat in the chair facing Lee's desk and adjusted his tie. He visibly took a deep breath, apparently trying to calm himself. "You were just supposed to keep her preoccupied, not marry her."

Oh, that. *"I know, and I intended to follow the plan. But well, somewhere along the way, I fell in love." He knew he sounded like an adolescent with a crush, but he couldn't help it. It was the truth.*

Melton stared at him with fire in his eyes and his expression cold.

Lee swallowed. This could go really bad. Was he prepared? Fired? Or worse?

A grin meandered across Melton's face and he snorted. "You old stud. I knew you were the best." He stood up, crossed to the side of the desk, and slapped Lee on the back. "My boy, it's time I move you up and out."

"What?"

"You've made more money for me than any other guy to come through here. I think you could make even more money if I placed you on your own. I'm setting you up in San Diego to run things permanently. I'm moving the rest of the office to New York at the end of the month. This tower will be yours. You'll be free to

hand pick your staff."

Lee was speechless. A rock of surprise anchored in his throat.

"I'm going to assume your lack of response is elation." Melton turned for the door. "Oh, and fire Don Crary."

Chapter Twenty-Four

"Aw, the great Freddy Big Bucks is living the good life," Bill said. "Even had to fire his own friend."

Fred faced the old man. "Why'd you pull me out? Things were getting good."

"I didn't pull you out. I'm just sitting here minding my own business." Bill sat on the floor in the corner with his legs spread wide apart and his robe wrapped around his thighs like shorts. On the floor in front of him were tongue suppressors stacked in the shape of a house.

"Right. Well, you said something, and now, I'm here." Fred slumped to the floor. "Did you see my beautiful fiancée? And my promotion at work?"

"So, things were good." Bill blew a raspberry through his lips. "Big deal."

Fred eyed him. "What do you mean *big deal*? It is a huge deal. I was at the top of my game. Life was sweet. Not many men have achieved what I did in that amount of time. I was the best."

"Significant tense...*was*. Your life *was* sweet. You *were* the best. Notice what those two words have in common? Or do you need to go back to grade school and learn your tenses?"

Fred crossed his arms. "Admit it, old man. My life wasn't so bad."

His companion peered up from the pile of sticks

and smirked. He rolled over to stand, knocking his house over in the process.

"Bummer." Fred hid a snicker behind his hand.

"So, back to how your life was good. You had cash flowing from your pockets, and a gorgeous dame agreed to marry you. All of that doesn't matter." He gestured to the body. "You weren't as great as you think, and we've already established you weren't all that happy."

Fred swiped at the air. "Whatever."

"So, did you fire your friend Don?"

"Collateral damage."

Bill sneered. "So, is that what you're calling friends today?"

The heat rose up Fred's spine. "Look, old man, in my position, I don't have the luxury to make friends. Some things are just more important."

"Yeah, I'm sure." Bill cocked his head to the side. "Do you know what today is?"

He shrugged. "Should I?"

"It's December 25th. Christmas Day, and you're here. If life was all peaches and cream," Bill jumped up on the footboard and pointed at the inert body, "...then what are you doing here, my friend? And where are the presents?"

****

The phone rang in the kitchen. Stan looked over his shoulder, debated if he should get it, but decided the answering machine would pick it up. Something wasn't quite clicking for him, and he didn't want to be distracted. What was the name he'd seen for ownership of the mansion where his father was shot? It wasn't Melton's—

"Hi, Stan, this is Kari."

Oh no, Kari. He looked at his watch. 5:30. He'd missed the Christmas ham.

"...I'm hoping you're all right..."

He leapt up from the floor, but his leg cramped. "Ouch! Oh man, I'm getting old." He limped as fast as he could into the kitchen, slid across the tile, and snatched up the phone next to the refrigerator.

It buzzed in his ear. *No!* What was her number? He flipped through a stack of papers on the counter. *Pizza, drycleaners, Bogan. No, Kari.* He pushed play on the recorder.

"Hi, Stan. This is Kari. I may be crazy, but I thought we'd agreed on meeting for dinner at five. I'm hoping you're all right. If you can, call me when you get this. Oh yeah, and Merry Christmas."

I'm a jerk. "Wait! You didn't leave a number." *I'm a big fat toad.*

"Why didn't you leave a number?" *Because I'm supposed to have it. Better yet, I'm supposed to be over there eating ham right this minute.* He walked to the bathroom and looked at his unshaven face and rustled hair. *Kari, I'm sorry I'm such a jerk.*

He jumped in the shower for a quick rinse. Ran a comb through his hair, threw on some cologne, and grabbed his travel razor. He found a pair of jeans crumpled by his bed and a sweater from his drawer. After he finished getting dressed, he grabbed the box of candy Bogan gave him, his car keys, and a case of "humble pie."

On the way to her house, he tried to free his thoughts of the case files. He would be in enough trouble without being scrambled. He pulled along the curb and glanced in the rearview mirror. *I look like a man who just woke up.*

Grabbing the chocolates, he stepped out of the car. The moon was high and bright in the cloudless sky, and the air warm, making Christmas in California once again like the Twilight Zone. He reached her entryway and breathed deep. *Please forgive me.* He rapped on the door and then stood back. Footsteps sounded, then a shadow passed over the peephole. A second later, a chain rattled, and she opened the door.

"Hi," she said. Her face revealed nothing.

"Kari, please forgive me. I was working on my father's case and lost track of time. When you called, I couldn't get up fast enough to grab the phone, and then I couldn't find your number. I'm really stupid and here's some chocolate." He thrust the red box out in front of him, feeling like a complete dope.

She glanced down at the candy, and a smile crept across her face. "Chocolate covers a multitude of sins. Come in."

She stepped back and allowed him to enter. The apartment had a loft feel. A table sat in the middle of an enormous room with wooden floors. A futon couch sat to the left and a kitchenette to the right.

"Is it too late to eat?" He laid the candy down on a table by the door and moved to remove his leather jacket.

"Not for you. For me, I kind of already did." She opened the fridge and pulled out a pan. The smell of cloves and pineapple filled the air.

"Would you like some help? I could fix my own plate."

"It's no problem. Besides, I may look thin, but I

have an incredible appetite. I'll eat again." She waved him in the direction of the table. "Go sit down. I'll just warm it up and be there in a moment."

He swayed from one foot to the other and then obeyed. A moment later, she joined him at the table with a plate filled with glazed ham, scalloped potatoes, and green beans laced with butter and almonds, then a smaller plate with just potatoes.

"Wow, this looks amazing. I've been alone for so long, I've forgotten what food looks like outside of a box or a can."

She laughed.

He brought a fork full of the cheesy potato mixture to his mouth and savored the bite. "Thanks for doing this. I'm really sorry to make you wait for me. I'm not usually a flake."

She sipped water from her goblet, her eyes fixed on his. So beautiful.

"Merry Christmas, Stan."

He smiled. "Merry Christmas, Kari. Thank you so much for being patient with me. My last girlfriend..."

She held up her hand. "How about we make a pact?"

"What's that?"

"I agree to make an effort to understand your crazy life and you agree to never talk about the women from before."

He nodded. "Deal."

She placed her cup back on the table and leaned forward on her elbows. "So, can I ask what you've found out?"

The notes flashed in his thoughts, sending excitement and confusion through his mind. He lifted his napkin from his lap and dabbed at the corners of his mouth. "I spent the whole night rewriting notes I saw on a fellow officer's desk. From what I can tell, Avarice has one link to the other murders. They had connections with the co-president of Melton and Gray, Asher Melton."

"So, does that make Melton your prime suspect?" She popped an almond in her mouth.

"No." He frowned. "He's dead."

****

Bill danced around the room, singing to the tune of *One Little Monkey*. "One little Freddy, dancing on the bed, was real stupid and got shot in the head. His companion called the doctor and the doctor said, no more Freddies dancing on the bed."

Fred clasped both hands over his ears. "Shut it, will you? You're giving me a migraine."

"You're spirit. You can't get a migraine." Bill licked his thumb and pretended to mount a horse. This time he sang to the tune of *She'll Be Coming Around the Mountain*. "Oh the dark lights a-coming, here it comes. Oh the dark lights a-coming, here it comes. Oh the dark lights a-coming—"

"Enough! Why do you have to be such a pest? Don't you have better things to do than annoy me? Isn't there some other guy in a coma somewhere in this hospital who needs your friendship more?"

The elderly man smiled. "I'm forever attached to you." He brought his hands together like prayer, bowed at the waist, and said in a mock Asian accent, "Aw, Freddy-son, you and I, we are one. One, you and I, are we."

Fred stood and flung his arms from side to side.

"No, no, no… When I wake up, I'll never see you again."

"Yes, but will you be waking up? Now there's the mystery of the year." Bill skipped from one end of the room to the other. "Wait. Rather for the decade. Yes, the decade."

Fred watched him dart from one end of the room to the other. It was like watching a tennis match. "You know, for an old guy, you sure do have a lot of energy."

Bill began singing again, this time to the tune of *Take Me Out to the Ballgame*. "Get me out of a coma, get me out of this room. Buy me a lawyer or coroner, tell me will I ever get back…"

The door opened, and Kari entered with an IV bag clasped in her hand. "Good morning, Mr. Avarice. How are you feeling today?"

Fred looked at Bill. "Why in the world does she ask me that every morning? It's not like I'm going to sit up and respond."

Bill rolled his eyes and looked back to her. "I think it's sweet."

The nurse pulled the empty bag off the pole and put a filled one in its place. "Well, I have some good news. Stan and I had our first date, and we have you to thank for it." She pulled back the top sheet and untucked it from the mattress. "He's just like me. A lone soul."

She crumpled the cloth and tossed it on the floor, then moved to a closet by the door and pulled out fresh folded linen. "He had dinner with me and then we talked about your case. He thought at first it might have something to do with a Mr. Mailman or something like that." She unfolded the sheet and flipped it up in the air.

It drifted back down on the body.

"Did she just say Melton?" Fred walked closer to her.

"No, she said Mailman." Bill snickered.

"Melton has to be the one." He couldn't believe it. They had found his shooter.

"The one?"

"The one who shot me. It would make sense. Though I don't remember precisely. But it has to be him." He turned to the nurse and tried to tug on her sleeve, but it went through her. "Kari, you've got to tell the detective that."

She tucked the sheet back around the end corners, whistling, oblivious to more than a sleeping body.

"Oh, why won't I wake up?" Fred felt trapped, like an animal behind glass.

"It torments him, you know?" Kari sighed. "I can tell. I'm sure if you had any family they'd feel the same about you." She pulled the blanket to his chest and folded the end over. "I hope he finds your guy. I hate to see you like this." She pushed a strand of his hair away from his forehead and behind his ear.

Fred was touched. She really did care about her patients.

"Bye, Mr. Avarice. See you later." She picked up the empty IV bag, tossed it, and left.

Bill sat on the black stool, looking back and forth from Fred to the body.

"What?" he said annoyed.

"You're both looking a little flushed."

"Stop it."

"Admit it. She takes good care of you."

Fred crossed his arms and leaned sideways against

the wall. "Yes, I suppose she does."

"However, you don't deserve it." Bill lifted his legs and pushed off the wall. The stool shot across the room and toppled over. He planted face first on the tiled floor.

His heart skipped a beat. Fred held out a hand to old man. "Are you okay?"

"Why? Do you care?" Bill winked and repositioned himself on the stool.

Fred let go of his hand. "Just be more careful, huh?"

"I think the mirror is working. The crazy coma companion can convey compassion 'cause coma client can compassion*ate*."

"Compassion*ate*? That's not even a word."

"Imagin*ate* with me, Freddy."

"Imaginate?" He sighed. "Unbelievable. I think it's time to go back to my past. I need a break from you." He walked back to the mirror and glanced over his shoulder. "I think there's something to be said about becoming a vegetable." Fred looked at the glass. "See you around, crazy old coot."

Chapter Twenty-Five

"Are you sure you want to go?" Lee knelt down and searched under the bed. His black loafer rested more than an arm's length away. He lay on his side and stretched. The tips of his finger grazed the heel. "These formal functions aren't all that fun."

"I want to go. It'll be fun to finally meet the people you work with." Elena stepped in the room dressed in a form-fitting, red silk dress. Her hair fell around her shoulders and a strand of rubies ornamented her neck.

Lee sat up and bumped his head on the bed frame. "Ouch!" He rubbed his head. "You look stunning."

She giggled. "You okay?"

He lifted his lost loafer and smiled. "Great. Ready?"

"Shall I ask the desk for a limo, or are we driving?"

"Call down for a car. Then we won't have to hassle with valets. They always frighten me with the way they handle my Porsche."

"We could take the BMW." She smirked.

"No, go ahead and call. Let's go in style." He walked into the bathroom just off the master suite and checked his reflection. A single wiry hair poked from his part. Great. He leaned close to the glass and plucked it. He winced and smiled. There. Perfect. He turned to go, when he noticed Elena standing behind

him, arms crossed, and an amused grin plastered on her face.

"First gray hair?" she asked.

"Don't be too smug, Mrs. Avarice. Your day is coming soon enough." He grabbed her around the waist and pulled her into his arms. "You do turn thirty this fall."

She placed a light kiss on his cheek. "Yes, but you've seen my mother. We Snow women age well."

"Why do think I married you?"

She pushed away and batted at him. "Very funny." She glanced at the clock on the wall. "It's ten till. We'd better get going."

Within twenty minutes, they pulled up to the red carpet in front of the Hotel Del Coronado. The driver opened their door and Elena gasped. "Look at the skyline, it's beautiful,"

Lee glanced up from the cufflink he was trying to fix. The sun had begun its dip in the Pacific Ocean, leaving a purple hue in its wake. "Uh huh. Come on." He guided Elena through the glass doors and into the Grand Ballroom. Philanthropists mingled with wealthy misers, swapping anecdotes and dull stories. Trays filled with caviar, salmon puffs, and cream-cheese rolls circulated from guest to guest. The well-to-do bantered with plastic smiles and polite handshakes, sipping champagne and white wine. Lee escorted his wife through the crowded room to where Asher Melton stood with a striking blonde on his arm.

"There he is." Melton stuck out his hand.

Lee offered a firm handshake and then directed his attention to Elena. "This is my wife, Elena. Elena, my boss, Asher Melton."

She smiled and offered her hand.

He held it for a moment, then regarded the woman next to him and let go. "This is my girlfriend, Krystal."

Elena shook her hand.

"Why don't we sit over there and talk." Melton pointed to a circular white leather couch away from the entrance. "Ladies, one of our customers brought a big display of jewels in the back. You're welcome to go check them out if our business banter gets too dry."

"Don't worry, we will," Krystal said, rubbing her hand over the back of his shoulders.

Lee stared at her. He couldn't help thinking she looked familiar, but he didn't know why. She had hazel eyes and high cheekbones, both saturated in cosmetics, and a voluptuous frame made more apparent by the taut sequin dress. Melton's trophy of the week.

A hostess brought them a round of drinks as they sat down and faced one another.

"This may sound odd, but you look familiar," Lee said to Krystal.

Her eyes remained on him as she took a sip of her champagne. "We met in the mailroom years ago."

"Oh, that's right." Not that he really recalled, but he hated to make a lower worker feel inadequate. After all, he started in the mailroom.

Melton put his glass on the small table and leaned forward with his hands clasped in front of him. "Excuse me, ladies, but I need to talk business for a moment." He eyed Lee.

"Here he goes," Krystal said.

Ignoring her, Melton asked, "What happened with the Conrad account?"

"She placed eighty thousand on the stock." Lee

lifted a finger to the waitress passing by. He placed his empty glass on her tray and took a fresh one. "I'm assuming she'll be worth triple that."

Melton rubbed his hands together. "We can cover eighty-K. But Gray wasn't thrilled with her reluctance. He thought it might be a waste of time."

Lee shook his head. "No, I don't think it will be. Just bear with me, and I'll make it happen. I promise."

His boss slapped Lee's back and then squeezed the base of his neck. "I will expect nothing less."

Lee gulped and forced a smile.

Melton looked toward Krystal. "Now, if you two will excuse me, I'm going to dance with my beautiful girlfriend." The two rose and moved to the wooden floor at the front by a stage. She wrapped her arms around Melton's neck and glanced at Lee.

What was it about her?

Elena rested her chin on his shoulder. "Your boss's girlfriend is a bit odd."

"Why do you say that?"

"I don't know, maybe because she keeps looking at you like she expects you to know her, but you don't."

"Do I detect a bit of jealousy?"

"No, just annoyance."

He watched Krystal sway in Melton's arms. Her body said she was Melton's, but her gaze said differently.

"Maybe if I hadn't plucked that gray hair."

Elena laughed.

Lee set his glass down and whispered in her ear. "You want to dance, Mrs. Avarice?"

Elena licked her lips and smiled. "Absolutely."

He led her to the dance floor and spun her around.

He was just about to spin her into his arms when a man in a wheelchair halted next to them.

"Clayton Gray?" Lee had never met the man, but had seen pictures and knew he had been crippled by polio at a young age. His appearance was the polar opposite of the ape-like Melton, but the power of Gray's pocketbook kept the vultures at bay.

Gray stuck out his hand and gave him a firm shake. "Nice to finally meet the infamous Lee Avarice. I hear you're a great asset to our company."

"Thank you, sir." Lee placed his hand on the small of Elena's back. "This is my wife, Elena."

He gave a slight nod, then looked back to Lee. "Keep up the good work, and I'll make it worth your while." A younger woman stepped behind him and took the reins of his chair. She whispered something in his ear, and he nodded. "Good night, Avarice." The woman wheeled him away.

"Good night, sir." Lee looked at his wife and smiled. "That was…"

"Clayton Gray. Yes, I heard." She grinned. "Seems to like you."

They began to dance again. "He should. I've made him plenty of money."

"Is that all he's concerned about?"

Lee glanced to where the man sat surrounded by a group of men in tuxes. "Notice he didn't even shake your hand."

She followed his line of sight. "Yeah."

"That wasn't an accident."

****

Stan sat in the plastic chair in the dark room, his legs kicked up on the footboard facing the comatose body. He'd hit another dead end. If Melton was dead and all signs pointed to him shooting Avarice, did that mean the shootings weren't related? No, that couldn't be it. They were all killed in the same manner, shot in the head in their offices in the early evening hours. The crime unit also determined from the bullets found in each body that the gun was a .45 caliber pistol with a silencer. But it just didn't make sense. Melton was killed the same way. It couldn't be suicide, because it was the same gun—a weapon that had yet to be found. He needed to figure out who else was connected with Melton.

He rocked in his chair, biting his thumbnail. The slight hum of the heart monitor and the rattling of labored breathing filled the air. An amber lamp outside the window supplied the room its dim light. He stared at the body in front of him. *The biggest mystery is probably why I like hanging out with a vegetable.*

Stan looked down at his notes and squinted. They weren't legible. He angled them toward the window. Black felt-penned letters were plastered across the page—who is connected to Avarice, Melton, and all the other tycoons?

He sighed. They cleared Melton's partner, Gray, two days ago. His son was the fourth person to die. Gray handled his grief for his son at the end of a noose.

"So, Fredrick Lee, anything you'd like to share with me that I haven't thought of yet?" Stan leaned back and stared at the ceiling. "Anyone I'm not thinking of?"

Silence.

"Yeah, well, when you're ready to talk." Stan dropped his feet to the floor and stuffed his notes in the briefcase by his chair. It was late and he had duty in the morning. He frowned. Of course, he'd be working on some other case.

The detective stared up to the heavens. "Rumor has it he isn't a nice man. Are you doing the world a favor by letting him sleep?"

The door opened and Stan jumped. It was Kari.

"Hi." He wiped at his eyes. "I'm just sitting in the dark, talking with our favorite patient."

Her hand moved to the switch on the wall, and the light sputtered on. "I see. Well, unless you want to see me give him a sponge bath, I suggest you get going."

Stan grabbed his briefcase from the floor and moved toward the exit. His heart lurched and he turned back. "Kari?"

Her eyes met his. "Yes?"

He set his case down, crossed to her, cupped his hand behind her head, and brought his lips to hers. Soft and warm. Electricity filled his body. He pulled back and gazed into her eyes. "Good night," he whispered.

She lifted her eyelids to half-mast, her lips in a dazed smile. "Good night."

He grabbed his briefcase, turned, and whistled all the way to the car.

Chapter Twenty-Six

The phone rang for the ninth time that evening. Lee glanced at Elena as she answered. From her reaction, the line must have gone dead at the word, "Hello."

She dropped the receiver and sighed. "What's the deal, Lee? Someone has been crank calling for weeks. Is there anything I should know?"

He laid the Wall Street Journal *in his lap and met her curious gaze. "Like what?"*

"I don't know." She perched on the couch armrest, arms crossed. "You always hear that if your husband is having an affair, there will be hang ups."

"I know where you're going with this, and you can stop right there. They hang up on me too." He took off his glasses and rubbed his eyes. "And I'm not having an affair. If some psycho has our number, then we'll change it. Okay?" He placed his glasses back on and scrunched his nose to straighten them.

She rolled onto the couch and stared overhead. The flames from the fireplace made flickering shadows on the popcorn ceiling above, and the crackling sound from the burning embers calmed the room. "Fine, I'll change the number in the morning. Because I'm tired of answering to static."

"Good idea." He flipped the paper open again and went back to reading.

She pulled the afghan from the back of the couch

and fluffed the pillow under head. She closed her eyes, stretched, and yawned. "Now to relax."

The phone rang.

****

"Good morning, Mr. Avarice," his secretary, Candi said. "You had some deliveries this morning. I've placed them in your office."

"Thanks." Lee opened the door to his office. He looked around, stunned. The room was filled with dozens of red roses. He glanced back at Candi.

She shrugged and smiled.

"Who are they from?"

"Secret admirer. I checked every one for a card."
She smiled again. "No luck."

He looked back at the flowers and grimaced. His wife wasn't going to be too happy, but if he kept it from her, she'd be furious. "Get my wife on the phone."

"Yes, sir."

"And hand these things out to all the women in the building."

She beamed. "Yes, sir."

Lee shut the door and crossed to his desk. At least ten dozen decorated the top alone. He placed the vases on the floor, just as the phone rang. He picked up his headset. "Hello?"

"Hi, honey. What's up?"

"Elena, don't get mad. Understand that I have nothing to do with anything that's happening." He closed his eyes and leaned forward, holding his forehead with his left hand.

"What now?"

"I have more than fifty-dozen roses in my office from a secret admirer."

Silence.

"Honey? I assure you, I don't know who it is." He opened his eyes and glared at the red haze.

"I'm in the building. I'll be right up."

"You're here?"

"Long story. I'll explain over lunch."

"But I have a lunch appointment."

"Not anymore."

The call ended. "Yep, I'm in trouble." He pushed the button on his intercom. "Candi, please get these roses out of here now."

"Yes, sir."

A moment later, she opened the door and began lifting the vases onto an audio/visual cart. "Are you upset?" his secretary asked.

"Yes, I don't know who is doing this, but it has to stop. My wife is getting jealous. And if you knew my wife, that isn't a trait she would normally have." Forking a hand through his hair, he peered out the window. Lights twinkled in the distance of the busy city. "As long as I've known her, she's been pretty easy-going. I want her to stay that way." He met Candi's stare with determination. "Do whatever it takes to find out who this person is."

"Yes, sir." She reached for another dozen, but her hip hit one on the cart. It started to fall. Lee leapt across the room and grabbed it at the same time she did. The two of them locked arms and laughed.

"Lee?"

He looked up.

Elena stood in the doorway, hands on hips, with an expression of fury.

He untangled from his secretary and stepped back.

"We had an accident."

"I can see that."

"Thank you, Candi. You can come get the rest later."

She nodded and wheeled the flowers out the door, shutting it behind her.

"Candi?" Elena's eyes narrowed. "That's a dessert, not a name."

Lee wiped off a few droplets of water on his suit. "Her full name is Candice. She goes by Candi."

"Fire her."

His head shot up. "What?"

Her eyes narrowed. "I said, fire her."

"I heard you. I just don't understand why." He stepped forward and reached out to embrace his wife. "Come on now. She's a hard worker."

She pulled away. "Someone wants you, and I can't do this."

"Come on, now." He brought her to his chest and kissed the top of her head. "I promise you, as soon as I find out who this is, I'll take care of them." He wiped the tear that trailed her cheek and lifted her chin to face him. "I love you, Elena."

He brought his lips to hers.

"I love you, too. Now, hire someone ugly."

"You still want me to fire Candi?"

"With a name not as sweet." She grabbed a handful of flowers, yanked them out of their container, and tossed them in the trash.

"You're serious?"

She glared. "Yes."

"But why? It isn't her."

"You don't know that." She snatched another

dozen and grabbed a pair of scissors off his desk. Cutting the buds into the garbage, she said, "Whether you can see it or not, that woman likes you. I trust you, but I don't trust her."

"This isn't like you. You've never been the jealous type." She reached for more roses, but he caught her hand and pulled her close. "What's going on?"

"I changed the number, but someone's still calling. Whoever it is has access to our information." Her hand cupped over his wedding ring. "I want to make sure we cover all bases."

He wrapped his arms around her waist, brought her head to his shoulder, and whispered, "Okay."

****

Vida Blaire sat across from Lee, dressed in a snug navy-blue suit. Her corpulent fingers rested high on her stomach. Whether or not she was the best person who applied was irrelevant; she possessed his wife's one requirement. She wasn't eye candy.

"I've checked all your references, Ms. Blaire, and it seems you come highly recommended." Lee scanned her resume. "When can you start?"

"I'm available to start on Monday."

"Well then, I'd like to offer you the job."

Her cheeks lit up in a huge grin. "That's wonderful. Thank you, sir."

"You can talk to human resources about pay and benefits. I try to stay out of those matters."

"They mentioned that in my first interview."

"Great." Lee stood and offered his hand.

She used the arms of the chair to stand and they shook hands. "Thank you again, Mr. Avarice."

He walked to the door and opened it. "See you

Monday morning at eight sharp."

She swung the strap of her purse over her shoulder and met him at the exit. "Good-bye."

Lee nodded, shut the door, and crossed to the bar. He was glad that was over. How he hated interviews— pretending to care and remain polite. Who needs it? He poured a glass of gin with soda and lay back on the couch. The soft cushion felt cozy, and he shut his eyes.

Just when he started to loosen up, the phone rang. Of course, now. He took one more sip and got up. "Hello?"

"Lee, I'm glad I caught you," Melton's voice came through the receiver. "I'm sending over an important client named Nell Renault. She has already invested a great deal of money in Melton and Gray. I want her to feel real secure with us. Understood?"

"Yes, sir. I understand."

"You do good on this one, and I'll make you partner."

His heart skipped. "And the stops?"

"Bankrupt in fourteen days."

"Yes, sir."

Lee hung up the phone and knocked back the remainder of his drink. He was going to be filthy rich.

****

"Freddy! Freddy, snap out of it!"

Fred blinked. "What?"

"Someone has been here."

Fred inspected the room. His unconscious body still lay like a corpse on the bed. The door was shut and the lights were out. "I don't see anyone."

Bill sat on the windowsill and looked out into the street. "A woman came by. She didn't say a thing. She just sat on the stool, looked at you for less than a minute, and then went on her way."

Fred glanced at the stool which sat less than a foot from the body. "She wasn't wearing a nurse's uniform?"

"No."

"What did she look like?"

A smile covered the old man's face. "Pretty."

"Do you think it was my wife?"

Bill shrugged. "How would I know? But from what I've seen, I don't think you'd have that much luck. She was too good for you."

"Could be my wife." Fred shot Bill a look. "Wait, you've seen my wife in the mirror. Did she resemble her? I mean, she'd be much older and have shorter hair."

His companion shrugged again. "All women look the same to me—blonde, brunette, redhead, they're all beautiful." He scratched his head. "She looked familiar though. I guess you could say her hair was shortish."

"Shortish? Another Bill-coined word?"

"Coined, yes. And you're welcome."

Fred raised one eyebrow. "For what?"

"For telling you about your visitor."

Fred huffed. "You pulled me out, when you could have told me later?"

"Nothing exciting was happening." Bill leaned back through the window, his spirit-persona translucent to the glass. "I'm not even sure why it was significant enough to show. But I suppose God had a reason to show you."

Fred sat down on a chair by the bed, kicked his legs up on the footboard, and clasped his hands behind his neck. "I figured it was the Ghost of Christmas Past."

"Dickens. Good author. Love him." Bill kicked off the sill and floated to the other side of the room.

"You're quite a literary man, aren't you?"

"Unlike you, I'm a cultured individual." The old man stood with hands on his hips.

Fred shook his head. "I'm convinced this is all a dream. I'm floating in and out of reality. Seeing things that are from my past, and you are just a being I've chosen to keep me company." He spanned his arms to encompass the room. "None of this is real. I'm not outside my body, taking trips into a mirror. I am my brain—"

Bill produced a raw egg from his coat and tossed it on the ground. "And that is your brain on the hospital floor."

Mouth gaping, Fred stared at the yellow goop oozing through the cracked shell on the tile by his feet.

"You were saying?" Bill batted his eyelashes with an amused grin pressed firmly in his cheeks.

"Where'd you get an egg?"

"Imagination, my friend." Bill pointed to Fred's head. "It's all in that gray matter you were just babbling about."

"So you concur? Our time together is nothing but my mind processing the past."

"No, not so sure about that." Bill scooped up the egg, lifted it to his mouth, and allowed the yoke to pour onto his tongue.

"Gross." Fred cringed. "Why not?"

Bill swallowed. "Because I know things you don't."

"Like?" He stepped closer to his companion, arms

crossed, expression tight.

Bill hopped around the room doing what looked like the Chicken Dance on crack. "Freddy Freddy, bo-betty, banana fanna fo feddy, fee-fine oh Freddy. Freddy."

"You're either brilliant, cantankerous, or just plain mad." Fred flopped to the floor, exasperated. He wanted out.

"You wanted to know why *I'm* here?" Bill laughed. "Because someone knows exactly what you need."

"What does that mean?"

"It means, my sleepy friend, that only a person with my personality could affect you."

"You mean, make me completely insane."

"Whatever it takes." Bill leaned back. "What did Paul say?"

"Paul who?"

"A great teacher." Bill lifted a finger in the air. "I have become all that I might save some, or something like that." He looked back at Fred. "Point being, someone, presumably God, doesn't want the darkness to take you, so I was sent."

Fred leaned his head against the wall and pinched his eyes closed tight. "He must have quite the sense of humor."

"He made you didn't He."

Fred peeked through his lashes. "I thought you angels were supposed to have compassion."

"Once again, I'm not an angel." Bill rested his chin in his hand. "And some people require soft loving care. Others, like you, need a brick to the head."

****

Stan pulled in his church parking lot and turned off

the engine. The pastor said he wanted to speak to him. Maybe because he hadn't been to service since his father died. He wasn't backsliding or any such thing, he just couldn't go. It hurt his heart.

"Well there he is," Pastor Ron said, sticking out his hand.

Stan skipped a few steps to greet him with a hand shake. "Hi, Pastor."

"Come on in. We'll go to my office. It's a little more private." He held open the glass office door for Stan to enter. "Mary Kay invited the women's group here to make sock puppets for the TJ orphanage. They're sweet women, but I wouldn't dare put you in that lion's den."

Stan laughed.

They entered the office at the far back, just left of the sanctuary. The walls were decorated with bookshelves and wood-carved Stations of the Cross. Ron motioned for him to have a seat on a leather loveseat.

Stan stared at the walls in fascination. He was drawn to the one with Christ in the Garden of Gethsemane. He sighed. "Your pictures are cool."

"Thank you. One of my best friends in college came from a Catholic background. He liked to carve and made them for fun." Ron took a seat in the chair facing him. "I liked them so much he gave them to me at graduation."

Stan faced him and tried to smile. He wasn't looking forward to the coming lecture. "So, I'm sure you're wondering why I haven't been in church much."

The pastor brought his hands together under his chin. "Yes, I've missed seeing you, but that's not why you're here."

Stan raised an eyebrow. "Really? Why then?"

"A new parishioner of mine—" He shifted forward in his seat. "Actually, she attended here a long time ago. Her husband has been shot, and she has asked for prayer."

"You want me to put her on my prayer list?" What did this have to do with him? He just wanted to get back to work. The sooner he did, the sooner he could go home and investigate his father's case.

"No, I think you might want to meet her. You and she are dealing with some of the same grief."

Warning signs flashed in his cerebrum. He put up his hands to hold back the matchmaker. "You just saved me from the lion's den, but you have a cougar in the wings?"

Ron chuckled. "I think she's the ex-wife of someone you know. Lee Avarice. Ring a bell?"

Now Stan wanted to kiss the man. "Yes, how can I contact her?"

"I can't give out personal information, but I do have her business card." The pastor reached in his desk. "Here. But remember, Stan, she wants prayer, not to be interrogated. So, don't make this all about you. I know you can't go near this case, but I thought if you were doing something for your church, it might help."

Stan gaped at the card in his hand. "Is this ethical?"

"It is if you have the right priority. Don't use her, Stan." He leaned forward. "Don't make me regret this, okay? I trust you to do the right thing."

No pressure. Stan stuck out his hand and stood.

Ron shook his hand. "Call me and let me know how it goes."

"I will." Stan walked to the door and turned back. "Thanks."

"I'll see you on Sunday?"

He pinched his lips and sighed. "I'll make an effort."

"Good."

He waved and left with the business card giving him a bit more step.

****

The mailbox on Lee's desktop indicated he had a new e-mail. He clicked the icon and the window enlarged. Another note from his mystery woman. He closed it just as the door banged open. He looked up.

Elena tramped in, jaw clenched, gaze sharp, cheeks flushed.

"You know I don't like you here while I'm working. I'm swamped. Let's meet for lunch later, okay?" He turned from the computer screen to the file on his desk, hoping she'd leave.

"Oh, no. This is business. You will talk to me now."

He looked up, not amused. Her face was flushed and her hair disheveled. "What's wrong with you? You look like you ran a marathon."

Her eyes snapped to his with distain. "I hear you're ready to close a deal with Nell Renault."

That got his attention. "How do you know about her? Her file is confidential."

"You know she's one of my good friends from high school."

"We've been married for over twenty years. I've never heard you talk about a Renault."

"Renault is her married name, and I call her

Ellie."

The light went on. Ellie had been a bridesmaid at their wedding and had attended several of their house parties. She was a nice woman. "Melton gave me her name." Lee went back to his file. "It wasn't like I sought her out."

Her palms slapped the desk. "You can't do that to her."

"I can and will," he said, without raising his head.

She came around the desk and bumped up against him. "She wouldn't give up her money so easily if she didn't trust you." She poked his shoulder. "Look, I know what you do. I learned from my mother ages ago. I have always hated it, but I've somehow rationalized it." She paced away from his desk. "I figured you were teaching people a lesson. Playing Robin Hood in some twisted way." She shot back around and pointed at him. "But Ellie is a good woman. She earned her money through helping others. Somewhere along the way, God has blessed her. Please, Lee. If there is any decency left in your soul, spare her."

Their eyes locked. A queasy feeling passed through his gut. Everything in him said to listen to his wife. But he couldn't, could he? Not if business meant anything to him. Not if he wanted to achieve his end game. "I can't."

"Can't or won't?" Tears brimmed against her lashes.

"You have no idea what my world is like." He stood. "You assume that just because I have my name on the door, that somehow I dictate what happens here." He walked around the desk and joined her. "I don't have any real power, Elena. I never have. But you

have things. Beautiful, wonderful things. You've never once questioned why you have them, and if you let this go, you'll continue to have them."

"I can't let you do this."

"You don't have a choice." He wiped the back of his hand against her wet cheek. "Just like I don't."

"We could walk away." Her eyes pleaded with his. "All these things, they don't matter. They're just stuff."

"You don't mean that."

"Yes, I do."

"You don't understand, Elena. I'm locked in. With this stop, I'll be partner. We'll be the richest couple in San Diego."

"And Ellie?" Her lip quivered. "She'll be devastated. Practically dirt poor."

"But we won't be."

Elena backed up slowly, shaking her head side-to-side. She glared at him as if snakes slithered from his eyes. "You didn't just say that."

"How can you look at me like that? I'm doing what is right for you and me. Isn't that what good husbands do?"

Her expression was heartbreaking. "Please tell me you won't go through with this horrible thing. Please."

Lee hated the answer, but it was the only one he had. "I have to."

"Then you are a monster," she rasped.

Lee laughed. "Don't be melodramatic, my dear. It's just money."

She wiped at the steady flow of tears on her cheeks.

"Here." He offered her a tissue from the coffee table. "You'll see it's not that bad."

She snatched it out of his hand with a puckered

brow.

He felt like a jerk but knew he couldn't give in to her demands. They needed this sale. Without it, he'd lose everything. And with it, he'd be everything. Compassion for his wife's feelings would make him lose his nerve. At the final quarter in the game, he couldn't afford a conscience.

"We can discuss it at home. Now is not a good time."

"No, we can't." She took a deep breath. "Because I'm leaving you."

"What? You can't be serious? This isn't about that admirer lady, is it? She hasn't called in months."

"No, Lee, this has nothing to do with her. This has to do with you." She extended her index finger at him. "If you don't call this off with Ellie, then I'll have my answer."

"And what is the question?"

She glared at him. "Whether or not you're still human."

Chapter Twenty-Seven

Stan ducked under the yellow tape and pulled on a pair of latex gloves and shoe covers. The doorman had said the majority of police had left a half-an-hour ago and the office now lay empty. Glass shards and cement residue covered the blood-splattered marble floor. He tiptoed around the outer perimeter of the lobby and down the hallway to where the crime appeared to have taken place. On the floor, in the doorway of the office, there was a taped outline of a body and a few yellow, numbered markers.

He pushed the door the rest of the way open and flipped the light switch. A fluorescent bulb flickered on overhead. The furniture lay in disarray. Chairs sat on their sides, papers littered the carpet, and books appeared to have been pulled from their shelves.

Shaking his head, he pulled a notebook and pen from his side pocket.

"Crazy, huh?"

He spun around. "Bogan. What are you doing here? You about gave me a heart attack."

"Sorry." She smiled, sporting a charcoal-colored suit and sunglasses. She set a case down, snapped it open, and withdrew a camera. "I'm assisting forensics now. Collecting evidence and bringing it back to their lab. My mentor is on his way up."

"You're switching departments again? What,

homicide get too boring for you?"

She stood and kissed his cheek. "No, you got too depressing for me."

"Funny."

A peculiar smiled played across her face. She looked him over.

"What?"

"You're seeing someone."

Butterflies flooded his stomach. "You're crazy."

With an amused grin plastered on her face, she reached to wipe her lipstick's red mark from his cheek. "Yeah, I can tell. Good for you. It's about time."

Trying to change the subject, he pointed to the chaos. "How about we work on finding out what happened here, huh?"

"You have to admit, I'm a great detective." She studied the room. "Any news on the vic?"

"According to the captain, he was alive when the cops arrived." Stan stared at a pool of blood in the carpet and snapped a picture. "No word on whether he made it."

Bogan nodded and dabbed her dark brow. Steps could be heard in the hall. "Must be my mentor, Shawn Jones."

"I know Jones. He's worked a few cases with me." He was a good guy, but also a by-the-book, no-nonsense cop. "Doesn't seem like *your* kind of partner."

Jones appeared in the doorway. "Hi, CSI."

Stan chuckled and snapped on some gloves. "That rhymes," he whispered to Bogan.

She smiled.

The man didn't.

Oh well. There appeared to be something under the

desk. Stan knelt and peered under the desk.

Bogan followed his gaze and snapped a picture.

A wallet. He lifted it carefully from the floor and flipped it open. "Scott Mueller. Age 42, 6'1, weighs 220."

"Friend or foe?" Bogan said.

Jones looked around the room and pointed to a plaque on the wall. "Friend. He's our vic." The agent held out a plastic bag and Stan dropped his find inside. "So, what's the story?"

"According to the custodian interviewed, the crime appeared to start as a lovers' spat. A woman came in and accused our victim of cheating. They fought, a gun was fired, and the woman vanished from the premises."

Jones squatted to the Berber carpet and used a pair of tweezers to lift a blonde hair. "Do we know who *she* is?"

Stan lifted a card from the edge of the desk. "Someone named Elizabeth Snow was here."

The man placed the hair in an envelope and then searched under the desk. "Well, the weapon was most likely a forty-five, similar to the one used in the tycoon murders."

Stan's heart skipped as he followed Jones's gaze. "How do you know?"

Jones reached out a gloved hand and lifted a shell casing. "I've helped with the investigation at all of the murders so far. When you've done enough serial murders, after about five or so, you start to get a feel for what the evidence says."

Stan knelt next to him and examined the gold casing in his gloved hand. "So, you think this was the same person?"

Jones met his eyes. "I can only speculate without the science to back me up, but off the record, yeah, I do."

"Then I'd rule out the lovers' spat," Stan said. Excitement streamed through his veins. He was on site for one of the tycoon murders. Maybe a thread of evidence, or in this case a strand of hair, could lead them in the right direction.

"But I thought the custodian said it *was* a lovers' spat?" Bogan asked. "Doesn't really fit the MO, does it?"

"People lie, get confused, misunderstand. I'm not about witnesses, I'm about the evidence." Jones walked around the room, placing yellow, numbered markers by the various evidence. Bogan trailed him, snapping pictures. "Most of the murders took place in someone else's office or home. Except for the first one, Lee Avarice, not one of the murders had occurred in the victim's own office." He swung his camera over his back and reached in his coat for a sterile Q-tip. He rubbed the end in some red goop on the bookshelf and handed it to Bogan. She poured a drop of liquid on the end. The tip turned positive for blood.

Stan walked around the desk and wrote a few notes. "Seems funny to me that a domestic fight would leave so many documents strewn around the room."

"Could have knocked some off the desk," Bogan said.

Stan shook his head. "No, the pattern suggests he or she was looking for something."

Jones picked up one of the sheets and held it under the desk lamp. "These are release forms for a screenplay."

"Not this one," Bogan said. "This one has the name of the first tycoon victim, Avarice."

Stan stepped around the desk and held out his hand. She handed it to him. It was a bill for the convalescent hospital Lee was staying in.

Bogan chewed on her bottom lip. "Do you think Ms. Snow knows Avarice?"

"Yeah," Stan said. "She's his mother-in-law."

"Do you think she tried to kill him?"

"The evidence will tell." Jones placed the plastic bags in a silver case and snapped it closed. "Well, I'm sure I'll be back." He looked at Stan and half-smiled. "I'll call the precinct when I have something."

"Do you think you could call me directly? I'd like to hear what you found out." Stan held out his card, hoping he would take it without question. If Jones called the main line, it would be passed off to the "brown-noser," and Stan would never know what was discovered.

Jones took the card and nodded. "Sure. Give me a few days." He turned to Bogan and beckoned. "Let's go."

"Did you get everything you need?" Stan asked.

"No, that's why I said I'd be back. I'm anxious to get this stuff to the lab."

Bogan hugged Stan and whispered, "You and I both know you're not supposed to be around this case."

"I know, but I'm begging you, Bogan"—he pulled back and looked in her eyes—"please don't interfere."

She slapped his shoulder and nodded. "See you, Heller."

"Bye."

The two of them exited, and Stan peered around

the empty room. A wave of despondency and hope clashed together in his heart. He prayed this was the break he desperately needed.

Chapter Twenty-Eight

Lee pressed the button on the visor in his car and the garage door lifted. He pulled in the opening and shut the engine off. A small bulb illuminated the quiet room. He considered staying there. Telling Nell Renault she was now broke was awful, but nothing would be as chilly as the reception awaiting him behind the wall in front of him.

He stepped from the car and slammed the door. It echoed in the vacant space. He pushed the button on the wall and the garage door closed behind him. The buzzing sound was deafening. Once it stopped, he entered the dark house.

"Elena?" He hit the switch in the kitchen, and the light flickered on. "Elena, honey, I'm home."

Silence.

With a quick toss, his keys landed hard on the counter. Lee grabbed a bottle of water from the fridge and listened to the house. Silence. Maybe she was upstairs. He unscrewed the lid, took a sip, before starting up the steps. The master suite was dark and quiet. Fumbling in the dark, he located and pulled the string below the ceiling fan. The room lit up. The bed was made. Her walk-in closet lay empty, except for a few hangers.

Where is she? *But he knew. Her dresser drawers were open and vacant as well. The other places where her shoes, make-up, and other things might have been— empty. Nothing. Another. Void. Again, he pulled one after another. He rushed to the bathroom and pulled open the drawers. Gone. Everything gone. She was gone. No! He grabbed a porcelain soap dish and threw it at the mirror. The glass shattered.*

His chest heaved, and his knees buckled underneath him. "I'm so sorry!" He sniffed. Wait! Did I just say that? I couldn't have.

****

Fred blinked. "I don't believe it!"

Bill glanced up from the medical modern art sculpture he was working on. "What?"

"I changed something." Fred started pacing, wringing his hands in front of him. "I really did."

"What? What did you change?" Bill hopped up and crossed his arms.

"I said I was sorry."

He squinted one eye like Popeye. "For what? You didn't do anything."

Fred batted at the air. "No, no. Inside my memory, I said I was sorry."

"So? Big deal. I say it all the time. Sorry, sorry, sorry, so sorry, I'm sorry."

Fred grabbed Bill by the shoulders. "I've never said I was sorry before."

"Are you sure? Because that's sad."

"Positive. Because I wasn't. I didn't care. You should be happy, old man. Something has changed in me. I miss my wife. And I feel remorse. Guilt. Why am I so happy? It feels awful."

Bill covered his mouth, obviously trying to hide a laugh. "I'm sure it does."

Fred wasn't amused. His eyes filled with tears. "I was so stupid. Completely, and utterly stupid."

"That's great." Bill sat back down with his creation.

"Great that I'm stupid?"

"Debatable, but no." He tossed a cotton swab in the air and made a slam dunk in the wastebasket by the door. "It's great you're starting to feel something. Welcome to the world of being human. Don't just visit...move here."

"Please be serious."

"Okay. If you could change anything, what would it be?"

"That's a no-brainer." Fred rolled his eyes. "Whatever it was that put me flat on my back in this comatose state."

Bill wrapped some gauze around a tongue depressor and held it to his face. "You got any gum?"

Fred flared his nostrils and glared.

"Sorry, I asked." Bill looked back to his project. "So, go on back in and change whatever put you here."

Fred ran a hand through his hair. "Unfortunately, I don't know what that is."

"Then start smaller. Anything else you'd change?"

"Yeah, things with my wife." He clasped his hands behind his neck and sighed. "I love her and blew it big time."

Bill flashed his gummy smile and leapt in the air like one might before starting a race. "Then go get her, tiger."

Fred didn't know how to do that. Was it even possible to change history? Or was this all some sick dream? "How do I return to a specific time?"

"Simple. Just think it."

It was worth a try. He walked back to the mirror and stared hard into the glass like so many times before. Only this time, he concentrated on the day he was first told about Nell Renault.

****

The phone rang.

It was Melton. "Lee, I'm glad I caught you. I'm sending over an important client named Nell Renault. She's already invested a great deal of money in Melton and Gray. I want her to feel real secure with us. Understood?"

"Sir, I'm sorry, but I don't feel comfortable taking her as my client." Lee cleared his throat. "She's my wife's friend, and if I want to stay married, then I can't do it."

"That's very disappointing." Melton's voice was flat, but Lee knew he was upset. He could picture Melton's face turning red.

"I understand," Lee said.

"She'll be calling you after lunch. Make it happen."

The phone went dead.

No way! It can't be. *Maybe fate was what it was. Fate. But he still had a choice, right? He picked up the phone and dialed his wife's cell number.*

"Hi, honey. We need to talk. Can you meet me for lunch?"

Chapter Twenty-Nine

Stan stared at the card on his kitchen counter. He'd picked up the phone five times already, but he couldn't seem to dial. When he was asked to call Lee Avarice's wife, the idea excited him. But after Pastor Ron's strict instructions, he felt less sure. Could he really pray for this woman? How could he resist drilling her? He tapped the counter and reached for the phone again.

The line rang. He willed for the answering machine to come on.

"Hello?"

Rats. "Hi." He cleared his throat. "Hi, I'm Detective—" He stopped. "I'm Stan Heller from your church."

"Yes, I'm sorry to hear about your father."

"You knew my father?"

"I attended a Bible Study of his years ago. We prayed for your family on Sunday."

Sunday? Of course, he hadn't been there. "Thank you." He shifted in his seat and readjusted the hand piece. "I spoke with Pastor Ron, and he thought maybe I could reach out to you and your husband."

"Do you know Lee?"

Do I tell her? "Sort of. I've visited him a few times in the hospital."

"Really?" She seemed surprised. "Well, I wish I could say the same. The truth is…we are divorced. I've worked hard to move on, and I can't bring myself to go backward."

"I wish I could say the same. I can't seem to get past my father's death. I believe Lee holds the key to something in this case."

There was silence for a bit of time. "I do appreciate your concern and the call. Pray for Lee. I would hate for him to slip away…" Her voice cracked.

"I will."

"Good-bye."

"Good-bye." The phone buzzed in his ear. That conversation did not go well. Why didn't he press for answers? *Because I wasn't supposed to.* Maybe he just needed to let go. Or better yet, go back to the hospital. There were no simple answers, but Lee held them, and Stan would get them.

****

Lee and Elena sat at Senora's Mexican Café munching on chips and salsa, listening to a Mariachi band a few tables over. When the musicians moved on, Elena leaned in. "Okay, what's wrong?" She didn't sound mad, just concerned. "You haven't invited me to lunch in ten years."

"I need your help. Melton is making me do something I can't bear to do." He reached his hands across the table and enveloped hers. "Though we've never really talked about it, I know you're aware that my business isn't always kosher. Usually, I can stomach it and move on. But now, Melton has asked me to betray someone who means a great deal to you." His voice cracked. His throat felt dry. He grabbed his ice water and guzzled.

With a fixed look, she watched him.

He placed the glass back on the table and inhaled in and out. "I tried to sway him, but he won't let me avoid this. If I walk away, he'll fire me or...worse." He wiped at the drops of sweat on his brow. "You don't know what he's capable of."

"Who is he trying to extort?"

He bit his top lip. "Nell Renault."

Elena didn't flinch.

"You don't seem surprised."

She withdrew her hands and began to toy with her wedding band. "I'm not. I already knew she was in bed with Melton and Gray. I have been trying to figure out how to talk her out of it without exposing you."

"You already knew?"

"Yes."

The waitress brought them two plates of fish tacos with black beans and Spanish rice. "Will that be all?"

Lee nodded, and she walked to another table. He squirted lime across the cabbage garnish, folded one of the corn tortillas, and brought the taco to his mouth. His stomach rumbled, but he didn't feel all that hungry. As delicious as it must be, it was like eating sand. He dropped it back to his plate and forced the bite down. "What can I do, Elena? You tell me what to do, and I'll do it."

"Quit."

The bite tried to come back up. He coughed, his eyes watering. He managed to swallow against the bile and grabbed for his drink. Sipping for a moment, he cleared his esophagus and managed to croak the words, "He'll kill me." He took another long drink of water and then looked at her. "Trust me, he won't hesitate to pull the trigger. And I don't mean that figuratively."

She raked the beans on the plate with her fork, eyes glazed over, mouth pursed.

He knew that look. The wheels of thought were moving, and she wouldn't stop until she'd reached a verdict. He waited.

"We'll pack up and disappear. You don't want this life anymore, right?" Her eyes searched his. "Because I don't want this life anymore either."

"We'll be poor."

"No, darling, we'll never be poor." A soft smile encompassed her mouth and eyes. "We have a wonderful savings built up, and I have my money from before we were married." She reached for the salsa and spooned some on her rice. "Besides you're brilliant. You were one of the youngest executives in the company. You'll get another great job in no time."

He took hold of her hand and brought it to his lips. "I love you."

"I love you, too."

He let go of her hand and sat back. "I hope you're right."

"What can go wrong?"

Chapter Thirty

The sun set, leaving the hospital room gloomy. Bill rested in the corner with his hands folded under his head.

Fred turned from the mirror and sat next to him. "I'm still here. Guess it didn't work."

Bill didn't respond.

The door opened and the silhouette of a woman appeared in the doorway. She crossed the room, her heels clicking on the floor. When she reached the chair by the bed, the light from outside the window shone on her face.

Elena?

"It's my wife." *It's really her. She's beautiful.* Her hair was shorter than he remembered. She looked a bit thin, but never had she looked so wonderful.

Bill sat up.

Elena scooted the chair next to the body's side and cupped his hand in hers. Stroking his skin, she began to hum. The soft sound of her voice soothed Fred's mind. *She's here. She came. Why now? Was it a coincidence? Did it work?*

"Lee, I'm so sorry. I should have come sooner. I've just felt so guilty." She leaned and kissed his forehead. "But I'm here now."

Fred glanced at Bill. "Guilty? Why should she feel guilty?"

"God, I really love this man." Elena's voice cracked. "Help him to find his way back. I need him in my life."

"She's praying." Bill clapped with excitement. "How wonderful."

Fred sat on the bed next to her, surprised. "Yeah, she hasn't done that since we first met."

"Dying kind of has that effect on people.

"I'm not dying."

"Yet." Bill winked.

She buried her head in the blanket and sobbed.

The door opened and Kari flipped on the light, startling Fred and Elena both. Fred backed away from the bed.

"Oh, I'm sorry. I didn't know he had a visitor. He hasn't had any other than the police." Kari took a timid step forward. "Are you his wife?"

"Yes." Elena stood and smiled. "I know it's strange I haven't visited before now, but I've been dealing with the guilt of putting him here."

Kari lifted her eyebrows.

"No, I didn't shoot him." Elena let out a nervous giggle. "Goodness no, I just meant it's my fault he got shot."

Kari checked the monitors and wrote a few notes on the chart.

Elena sat back down and looked at the body. "In order to save my friend from losing everything, I advised my husband to quit his job. He did…and look what happened." She broke down crying.

Fred grabbed Bill and kissed him hard on the cheek, laughing giddy.

Bill wiped his face with the back of his hand.

"Don't contaminate me."

"It worked! It really worked. I can do this. I can change my destiny. I can fix my mistakes." He ran back to the mirror with elation and an ounce of hope. "You were right, old man. There is such a thing as miracles."

"You're still in a coma, Fred." Bill nodded to the body. "Or didn't you notice that I'm still here and your body is still there?"

"Ah, yes, I know. But that's just because I didn't go back far enough." Fred lifted his pointer finger in the air and looked into the glass. "I'm going back in. And this time, I know where."

****

The morning mail truck backed up into the open bay door. Mike sat buried in envelopes. "Hey, Lee, can you get this?"

Lee nodded, got up from the card table, and grabbed the clipboard from the nail on the wall. "Hey Charlie," he said, reaching the man in the blue uniform. "How much do you have for us today?"

"Two buckets and a box." Charlie rolled the door on the back of his vehicle and reached for a plastic tub filled with white envelopes.

Lee stepped forward, took one of the buckets from him, and walked it over to a counter filled with cubbies. He then turned for the other tub.

Charlie placed the package on the card table and nodded. "You going to the game on Friday?"

"Maybe, if I get out of here at a decent time." He signed the clipboard and placed it back on the nail. "Your old lady going to let you go this time?"

Charlie laughed. "She'd better. I got her tickets to some chick show at the Civic Theatre."

"Smart thinking."

"You going, Mike?" Charlie glanced at the husky guy shooting letters through the postage machine.

"Nah, got other plans."

He rolled the door back down on his truck and waved. "See you tomorrow."

"Sure thing." Lee looked at the package on the table. Mr. Garret. He'd take that up first and then sort.

"Excuse me," a female voice said behind him.

Lee turned around.

A gorgeous blonde dressed in a red suit greeted him with a flip of the wrist, extending an envelope between two fingers. "I need this sent overnight. Can you handle that?"

He ran his tongue across his teeth and forced a plastic smile. "I think I can."

Her eyes narrowed. "Do you know who I am?"

He didn't answer her. Though there was something familiar about her.

Coolly, she removed a strand of hair from her eyes. "Melton's girl."

Lee wasn't all that impressed. He stared at her revealing no expression.

"Just make sure it's mailed, okay?" She glanced at his hands. "And make sure you don't get any of your filth on the outside. Wash your hands first." She set the letter on the counter and walked away.

"Sure." Lee rolled his eyes. "She's a piece of work."

Mike laughed.

"I have a package for Garret." Lee grabbed it off the table and started for the elevator. "I'll be back in ten."

Mike waved a hand in the air without looking up.

Lee took the elevator to the first floor. He stepped off and walked across the tan marble floor to the gold elevator for the suites above. He pressed the up arrow and waited.

The door opened. Two men dressed in well-tailored black suits looked past him. Lee stepped in and the door slid closed.

"I'm just saying Melton isn't going to be happy with you. You messed that whole thing up on a priority-one job," the man to Lee's left whispered. "You have to know when to do the stops. If you don't, they walk away loaded and you'll walk away a dead man."

The other man sighed. "I don't know if I'm cut out to be a con man. I'm just not good at it."

Lee shifted from one foot to the other. His ears burned with curiosity.

"Look, just tell the lady she's going to be rich. That's all you have to do. Then the job will be complete. As far as the client is concerned, what happens after that is beyond us. We can't control the market, right?"

"I did that. It's not that simple."

The bell dinged, and the door opened. Lee didn't move. The door slid closed, and he turned to face the men. Tension filled the tight space.

"I'm sorry to eavesdrop—"

"Then don't," one man said.

"The success to any con is making the person believe in you." Lee smiled. "It's not enough to just tell them they're going to be rich. You have to build their trust."

The elevator stopped again and the door opened.

The men looked up at the floor number and then moved past him without a word.

Lee sighed and pushed the ninth floor again. He still loved the rush of that moment. Telling those guys. Wait! Oh why didn't I stay quiet? *He was here to change things, but now Melton would call him into his office and offer him a promotion.* Why didn't I keep my mouth closed this time? *He didn't want to have to say no to Melton, but now he would. If he wanted his body back, he'd have to say no.*

He delivered the package to Garret's secretary and then returned to the basement.

It wasn't a surprise that his boss, Fenton, waited for him outside the elevator. "You're wanted on the thirteenth floor. Mr. Melton wants to see you."

"Okay." Lee turned back to his ride and sighed as he began the ascent.

The elevator door slid open, revealing a cherry-wood island in the middle of an open, green marble room. A woman sat behind the desk. "Can I help you?" she asked.

Lee tried to smile. "Yes, I work in the mailroom. I was asked to come see Mr. Melton."

"Your name?"

"Lee Avarice." He handed her his badge.

She looked from the plastic ID on his chest, then to his face. "Fine, have a seat and I'll buzz his secretary."

Lee sat on a padded bench to her left. If he didn't turn down the position, in a few years, this lobby and office building would be named after him. But to what end? The carpet was now stained with his blood.

"Mr. Avarice?" the receptionist said.

Lee looked up.

"Mr. Melton will see you now."
****

Stan tapped his pen in rapid motion on the arm of the chair at the end of the captain's desk. The boss was late for his debriefing. Outside the glass room, Stan heard laughter. *How long since I joined in the precinct's pranks and merriment?* Now the department members avoided him. Bogan once told him they assumed he'd be angry or offended at their jokes. They were probably right. He wasn't the fun guy from before. He was tainted with bitterness and revenge— emotions he himself despised. They were embarrassing.

His cell rang in his pocket. He pulled it out and snapped it open. "Heller."

"Good morning, Officer. This is Nurse Hill at Mercy West. You left a message about the possibility of seeing our patient, Scott Mueller."

Stan sat up in his chair. "Yeah, thanks for calling me back."

"I'm sorry, sir. But he died on the operating table."

Stan closed his eyes. "Thank you again." He snapped his phone closed and stuffed it in his pocket. The door banged open and he jumped. The blinds clanged and swung side to side.

"Sorry, I'm late," the captain said, as he positioned himself in the high-backed chair behind the desk. "I got stuck fighting with the D.A. over some drug bust." He folded his hands on the desk and looked at him. "You ready?"

"Yep." Stan handed the captain his folder and swallowed. "Everything is in there."

The captain took the file and flipped through it. He peered at Stan and went back to reading. His expression hardened. *Here it comes.* His eyes slid up from the file to meet Stan's. They narrowed. "This is about a tycoon murder."

Stan shifted forward in his seat. "I didn't know it until I got down there. CSI collected evidence that connected it to them."

The captain clicked his tongue on the roof of his mouth and closed the folder. "I'll give it to Kessler. You can get busy on the bus stop homicide from last Tuesday. Potter needs to take some personal time and can't finish it."

Stan jumped up. "No, Captain, please. I've spent at least twenty man-hours on this case."

"And I'm sure twenty dozen more on the tycoon murders. Doesn't mean I'm going to change my mind. You're not allowed near that assignment...even if it pertains to the one you're already working on."

Stan slumped in his seat. "I understand your reasons, but you and I both know that if this wasn't personal, I'd be the one conducting this investigation."

The captain folded his hands on the desk and leaned forward. "There's no doubt you're an amazing detective. You see things on a level most cops don't understand after a lifetime on the force." He took a deep breath through his mouth and exhaled through his nose. "But there's no way I'm putting you near a case that has to do with the tycoon murders. Believe it or not, I'm protecting your career." He leaned back and pointed to the door. "Now go hand all your notes to Kessler." A slow grin formed across his face. "Before I fire you."

Stan stood, heat rising up his neck. "Fine!" He walked to the door and thrust it open.

"Heller?"

He faced the captain.

"I'm sorry."

Stan nodded and slammed the door behind him.

Chapter Thirty-One

Lee stood outside the carved wooden doors that led into Melton's office. The blood seemed to have moved from his head to his stomach. He felt faint. He inhaled and knocked.

"Come in."

He pressed down the handle and pushed the door open. "Hello, sir." His belly flipped. His hands were shaking. He opened and closed them, willing them to settle down.

Melton stood. "I won't bite, Mr. Avarice. Come closer so we can talk."

He walked forward and stood within ten inches of the mahogany desk. The man seemed bigger than Lee remembered.

Melton's eyes skimmed over Lee's frame, probably sizing him up. "Please sit," he said, waving to the high-backed leather chair in the center of the room.

Lee glanced at the chair, back to Melton, and then took a seat.

His boss came around the desk and sat on the corner facing the chair. He folded his hands and smiled. "It's been brought to my attention that you've been talking to my brokers about misleading my customers."

Spit caught in Lee's throat and he swallowed. "I'm sorry, sir, I just overheard them talking in the elevator, and I offered them an alternative plan."

Melton pressed his lips together and nodded. "I see. And what is it you overheard?"

Lee stared down at his hands. "How to con some lady out of her inheritance."

"And you offered them some advice?"

He looked up and caught Melton's gaze. "I know I shouldn't have said anything. I just blurted out what came to mind."

Melton walked back to his desk and opened a red folder. "Your real name is Fredrick. Why do you go by Lee?"

"Am I am in trouble, sir?"

Melton didn't flinch. "That all depends."

"On what, sir?"

"On whether or not you are honest with me." Melton reached into a drawer and withdrew a bottle of scotch and two tumblers. "Drink?"

Lee drank often, but the thought of liquor just then made his stomach hurt. He shook his head.

The big man shrugged and poured himself a drink. "I'm a powerful man, Mr. Avarice. I know more than you can imagine. So, it would be within your best interests to level with me. When I ask a question, I expect an answer." He leaned in. "The right one."

Lee sighed. "I ran away from home when I was just a teenager. I used my middle name in order to keep my aunt from finding me. I figured, if she was asking around for a Freddy, no one would think of me."

"Very good." Melton swallowed the amber liquid. His eyes watered a bit, but he didn't seem to mind. "Tell me what you told my men in the elevator."

Lee shifted in seat. "I just told them the key to any

con is building trust."

Melton raised an eyebrow. "And how would you know?"

"I, um—" He cleared his throat. "I used to con people out of money in school. It's how I was able to run away."

"I see. And how much did you con?"

"It took me about five years, but my final amount was four thousand, five hundred, eighty-two dollars." Lee smiled. "And twenty-seven cents."

Melton leaned forward. "That's almost a hundred a month. Not a bad plunder for a kid. I'm impressed." Melton leaned forward. "Well, how would you like a promotion?"

Lee somehow hoped this moment in time would have changed. That instead of just being surprised and honored, he'd be repulsed. But despite his perfect hindsight, Lee felt himself sucked in. "Me?"

"I'm about to reveal something to you, Mr. Avarice, but before I do, you're going to sign a contract for me." Melton pushed the intercom on his phone. "Miss Myers, please bring in a H.E.L. contract."

I can't do this. *If he did this, he'd forever be locked to this man. A man who would one day try to kill him.*

Melton turned back to Lee. "I need an answer. Do you want to be promoted?"

"Well, I know I don't want to stay in the mailroom."

He slapped his hands together and moved to pour himself another drink.

"But no." Lee's heart raced. "I'll have to decline."

The door opened, and the petite woman with red hair entered with the blue document. She sat it on the desk in front of Avarice.

Melton's eyes locked with Lee's. He didn't look at his secretary, as he said, "Thank you, Miss Myers."

She turned and left the room.

"You don't know what you're saying, Mr. Avarice. I'm offering you a great opportunity here. You're looking at about fifty-K a year to start." He pulled a gold pen from his jacket pocket and held it out. "Doesn't that sound good? Or do you like working in the mailroom?"

Lee scooted forward in the chair. "I'm sorry, sir. But I have other plans." He stood and walked to the door. "Thank you, though. I appreciate the opportunity." He didn't look back. Couldn't look back. A haze of fear clouded his vision. He scurried to the elevator and pressed the button several times. The number above the elevator clicked at each floor. He glanced back at Melton's door, fearful. It didn't open.

The elevator arrived, and he stepped in. A realization washed over him. He'd have to quit. If he stayed another day, things could get unpleasant.

Chapter Thirty-Two

Fred dropped to the tile floor, exhausted.

"You're still here?"

He shot around to face the old man.

Bill grinned from his favorite stool, clutching an empty roll of toilet paper. "Welcome back."

How can this be? Fred stood up and walked to his body. "I don't understand. I did it. I quit. I said no to the boss man. Didn't it work?"

Bill waddled to the edge of the bed, with the stool between his legs, and rested his chin on the body's shoulder. "Looks to me like you didn't change the *right* thing."

Fred paced, rubbing his temples. "I don't understand. I just don't. I'm sure Melton shot me. He should have been out of my life for good."

"Well, one person isn't in your life anymore."

He stopped and looked at the old man. "Who?"

"Notice your wife is gone?" Bill's eyes darted back and forth in his sockets.

Fred stopped. "Maybe she went to get something to eat."

"Nah. She vanished. I saw it with my own two peepers." Bill jumped up and spanned the room with his arms. "Poof! Into the abyss." He flailed his arms in the air and spoke in an old-English accent. "Gone with the wind, she was. To and fro, to and fro, doth the lady

197

disappear? No longer is she linked to this male of her affection, but gone hither to her life before."

Heat flooded Fred's face, and he narrowed his eyes. "What are you babbling about, grandpa?"

Bill raised two fingers in the air in the form of the peace sign. "She's like gone, dude."

"Oh no!" Fred's mouth dropped open at the realization. "I never even met her."

"That's a strange marriage."

"I met her because of a business deal through Melton and Gray. If I never worked for them, then I would never meet her mom, which means I would have never met Elena."

Bill sat next to him and placed an arm around his back. "Then go back in and change that too."

He shook his head and pulled away. "Why should I? I'm making these changes and it isn't helping. I'm still in a coma and now I'm without my wife."

"One change made her come back and another took her away. Choices we make in life can alter what happens, but sometimes we still have the power to fix those mistakes."

Lee pursed his lips. "You know, for a crazy old coot, you sure have an ounce of wisdom."

Bill leapt to his feet. "Only an ounce? Ha!"

"You know what I mean."

Mumbling to himself, Bill sat on his stool. "Reservoir is more like it. Vast quantities. Immeasurable amounts. Infinite masses."

Fred tuned out Bill's ramblings and surveyed his body. His flesh-shell lay so still, with a countenance void of life. In great contrast, his mind was active and sound. Ironically, in order to maintain the ability to think, his body needed to remain on machines. "What would make me continue to stay in this state? If I have the mental desire to wake up, why don't I?"

Bill scratched his chin. "Maybe desire isn't enough."

"Yeah, what is?" Fred met the old man's eyes. "What is enough, Bill?"

"Finding your way. Your body's ability. Who knows? God, I suppose."

"How long?" Fred sighed.

"A few hours, days, years. Whatever it takes." Bill turned away and went to stare out the window.

Fred paced. *A few years? No way.* He had to stop fighting this and think. Why was he still in a coma? "Why do you suppose I'm still laying here? Why didn't quitting Melton and Gray stop my journey to the gurney?"

Bill laughed. "Journey to the gurney. I'm a poet and my feet know it, because I'm a Longfellow. Ha! You've been hanging around me for too long."

"I concur." He couldn't help returning Bill's smile. There was something magical about the man. One moment, Fred wanted to toss him out the window; the next, he wanted to hug him. "My problem, Bill."

The old man nodded. "Okay, first things first. You said Melton shot you."

"Yeah, that's right."

"Well, he knew about your conversation with the guys in the elevator. Maybe he took you out for *that* reason?"

"Smart, Bill. Very smart."

He looked down at his fingernails and wiped them on his shirt. "Well, ah, I would have said brilliant."

"And humble." Fred laughed. "Today, for the first time, I like you, old man."

"That's because you're an idiot."

Fred raised his left eyebrow. "I'm an idiot for liking you?"

"No, for taking so long." He winked and disappeared behind the curtain on the other side of the room.

Fred shook his head and ambled to the mirror. He was going back to the past and reuniting himself with Elena and his body.

****

Kari appeared from her bedroom dressed in a cream-colored, lace dress with spaghetti straps. Her hair was pulled back, with a rhinestone headband, and a cross-diamond necklace lay against the nape of her neck. His breath caught in his chest. *Gorgeous.*

"You look beautiful," Stan said.

She sized him up and smiled. "You clean up good too, Detective." He wore his favorite charcoal-colored suit and a black tie, and had splurged on a trip to the barber for a haircut and a clean shave.

He smiled. "You ready?"

She reached for a sweater on the end of a rocking chair and motioned to the door. "Let's go."

In the car, exultant nerves invaded his stomach, but he hadn't been this content for a long time. The smell of vanilla and soap lingered in the air. He closed his eyes and breathed it in before starting the car.

"Where are we going?" she asked.

He pulled his seatbelt on and flicked his blinker. "It's a surprise."

"A surprise, huh?"

He glanced at her and smiled. "We've been friends for almost a year now. I think it's time we celebrate."

She offered a grin and glanced out the window.

The lights from the city traffic lit the car. He saw the disappointment on her face. He had said the "F word"—friend. Sure he could remedy it, but in a sick way, this made it better. She'd never know what hit her.

He pulled the car into the parking lot of Benvenuto Pizza and turned off the engine. He stepped out and around to the passenger side to let her out. As he opened her door, he said, "I hope you like Italian food. They have the best pasta in all of San Diego."

"Love it." She grabbed her purse from the floorboard and joined him.

The hostess sat them in a booth in the back. Red votive candles on lace tablecloths lit the room. While Kari scanned the menu, Stan stared at the velvet box in his palm in his lap. *Is this crazy? Am I?* He'd only known her a year, but she was perfect for him. Before her, his heart had stopped pumping. She brought him back to life.

"I think I'll have the chardonnay shrimp pasta." She laid her menu on the table. "What about you?"

"That sounds great, but I'm a lasagna man."

She smiled and met his eyes.

He cleared his throat and opened his mouth to speak, but the waitress appeared poised to take their order. "What can I get you?"

"Chardonnay shrimp pasta for the lady, and lasagna for me." He looked at Kari. "Would you like a pitcher of root beer?"

She nodded.

He glanced back at the waitress. "A pitcher of root

beer and some of your cheesy bread, with a side of your special sauce."

The waitress collected the menus and walked into the kitchen.

Stan turned back to Kari. Her eyes sparkled in the dim light. No longer nervous, he said, "Kari, I couldn't have survived this year without you. I believe you were brought into my life for a reason."

"Like you said, we're good friends." She grinned.

"No, you mean more to me than that." He took her hand in his. "I love you." He slid out of the booth and knelt next to her on one knee. "I love you with all my heart. If you'll have me, I'd like to be your husband. Kari Jensen, will you marry me?"

Tears filled her eyes. She brushed her lips against his and whispered, "Yes."

Chapter Thirty-Three

*There she is. Lee stood outside the theatre waiting
to see Elena. She wore a strapless black dress and her
hair fell in soft waves around her bare shoulders. He
couldn't wait to touch her again. She was so close. He
moved out of the shadows to approach her.*

"You ready to go?" a man said next to her.

Lee stopped.

*She smiled and kissed the man on the cheek.
"Absolutely."*

What? Lee stood on the side of the road, stunned.
Who is her date? *It was supposed to be him. How could
there be another man? He followed them to where they
stopped to unlock a gold Porsche. He knew that car.
Under the streetlight, Lee got a better look at the man.
It was his old friend. Don must have taken his spot at
Melton and Gray. Beth Snow must have forced him to
take Elena out instead. It made sense. Lee looked at the
ground, biting his thumbnail.* Think, Lee. Think. How
can you turn this?

"Excuse me. Can I help you?" Don said.

*Lee looked up. Both Elena and Don stared at him.
"Uh, no. I just lost my car." He scanned the parking
structure and then looked back to the couple. "Hey, do
I know you?"*

*The man didn't look amused. "I doubt it." He
turned to Elena and nodded to the open door. "Get in."*

Lee stepped forward. "Sure I do. You're Don Crary. We used to work together." Hang on. Don was a broker and wouldn't have known a guy in the mailroom. *"I used to bring you your mail."*

Don laughed and slammed the door shut. "Sorry, I don't remember you."

"My name's Lee Avarice."

A connection sparked in Don's eyes. "I thought you were dead."

A fist of emotion socked him in the stomach. "Why would you think that?"

Don shrugged. "Rumor had it you were shot."

"I was."

"And what do you want with me, Mr. Avarice?"

"Nothing. I told you. I'm just looking for my car."

Don eyeballed him.

Lee let out a nervous chortle. "I know it's embarrassing to admit but haven't you ever lost a car?"

The man averted his eyes to the passenger side of the Porsche, obviously considering his date. "Good luck, Mr. Avarice. Glad to see you're okay." He walked to the driver's side.

"Thanks. See you."

Don climbed in his car without another glimpse. The engine revved, and the tires squealed out of the lot.

Lee bent to the pavement and tried to slow his breathing. Don had just confirmed his gravest fear. A hit was put out on his life for knowing too much.

****

Nurse Kari pushed a needle in the body's right arm. Red liquid seeped from his vein and into the glass tube. "Guess what, Mr. Avarice?"

Silence.

"Stan asked me to marry him." She snapped the rubber tourniquet from his arm, leaned down to his ear, and whispered, "And I said yes." She sat the glass tube on the tray next to the bed, while holding pressure on the wound site, and placed a Band-Aid where her finger had been. "I can blame you, you know. If you hadn't gone off and gotten yourself shot, I wouldn't be picking out flowers and china patterns." She beamed. "You are now officially my second favorite person in the world, and you've never even talked to me." She pulled the covers down to his knees and pulled his gown back. "I know this is unpleasant, but I need to check you out." She tipped him a bit to the side, revealing red, oozing sores on his back.

"These aren't looking good. I'm going to have to bring the doctor in." She laid him back down and pulled the covers to his chest. "I know you hate it when the white coat comes to see you. It always means poking and prodding. But you're a big man. You can take it." She lifted the paper on the top of his chart and wrote some notes. "Well, I just wanted to thank you for being such a good friend to me this last year. You always let me talk, and you never interrupt." She laughed. "If you could walk, I'd make you my mister of honor—if there is such a thing." She patted his shoulder, slipped his file in the slot on the end of his bed, and left.

"Okay, now she's just making fun of me," Fred said.

"I don't think so. I think she's just happy." Bill shook his head and smiled. "After all this time, she's getting married. That's wonderful."

Fred sat on the floor and bent his knees.

"Wonderful."

Bill frowned. "You don't seem very happy about it."

"If I leave things as they are, then they'll get married and live happily ever after." He rested his chin on his knees and sighed. "But if I do that, then my life will forever stink."

"You think they won't be together if you change things?" The old man traveled to where Fred sat.

"If I can figure this whole thing out, then Stan's father won't have to die. More importantly, I won't be in a coma. Detective Heller will never have had my case and never had a reason to visit here. Stan and Kari will never have met."

Bill squatted next to him. "Oh."

"Yeah, tough decision."

He raised an eyebrow. "For you?"

Fred half-smiled. "I guess you're getting your way. I'm cultivating a conscious."

"Best news yet."

Fred shook his head. "I have to go back in."

"Yeah," Bill wrapped his hands behind his head. "But do you know where to go?"

He took a deep breath and exhaled as he spoke. "I want my wife back."

****

Lee sat on the bench where he proposed to his wife many years ago, and where they'd gone on their second date. The art exhibit was for one day only, and he was sure Elena wouldn't miss it.

He arrived one minute after the doors opened and they would close in less than three. He hoped he was right, and that Don wouldn't be with her. He knew Don.

The man hated art.

A small girl with ponytails and a yellow dress smiled at him and ran ahead to find what appeared to be her mom. A man dressed in black dungarees spent ten minutes with his face inches from a huge statue of a bug, and a woman with a sketchpad sat across from him staring above his head at a big red dot.

He glanced at his watch and sighed. Where is she? *Maybe he'd been wrong about her.*

No, there she is. *Just as he remembered her.* Beautiful. And alone. *He stood up and followed close behind her. She ambled the hall from piece to piece, studying each one in detail. When they reached the main exhibit, Lee dropped his keys next to her foot. She reached for them at the same time he did, and they bumped heads.*

"Ouch! Sorry," he said.

She held her head. "Me, too."

"You okay?" He picked up his keys and stuffed them in his jean pocket.

"Yeah, I'll be fine." She smiled. "You?"

He returned her smile. "Never better. Maybe I'll even be smarter. Able to enjoy this…art."

"You don't take pleasure in modern art, huh?"

He shook his head. "I'm more of a Rembrandt, Monet sort of man. I guess I'm not much for the unexplainable."

"Prefer steak over salad." She laughed and let her gaze wander around the displays on the walls of the room. "I don't know why, but I love all art—even this stuff."

"I guess I might if I understood it more."

She stared at him for a moment.

207

"What? Do I have something on me?" He wiped at his face.

She laughed again. "No. I just get the feeling I know you from somewhere."

"Huh? I was thinking the same thing. Weird." They stared at each other for a long moment and then he deliberately looked at his watch. "Well, I should probably leave you alone. Let you get back to enjoying..." He glanced at a statue that looked like an upside down monkey on a stick. He laughed. "Whatever it is you're enjoying."

She glanced at his wrist. "Do you have somewhere you're supposed to be?"

"No, I just don't want to bother you."

She shook her head. "No bother. Let me give you the proper tour. If you still hate it after I've explained it, then you're hopeless." She grinned with a spark of mischievousness in her eyes.

"Deal."

She held out her elbow and he looped his arm through hers. They moved through the museum looking at splashes of paint, stacks of metal, and carved shapes. If it bore the label "absurd," it was in this building. Lee had been there before, so none of it surprised him. But he did recall laughing inside the first time he came. It was before he loved the woman on his arm and had a real chance to be with her. On their second date, he was still a con man on the job.

A man in a gold coat walked toward them. "The museum will be closing in a few minutes."

Lee and Elena nodded and exchanged glances.

"Well, I guess that's it," Lee said. "I had fun, despite the psychotic environment."

"You're a good sport."

"You're a good guide."

"I know this may be a bit forward, but would you like to get some coffee?" Elena asked.

It was as if their dates had been reversed. "Yeah, I'd love to."

"There's a coffee shop just around the corner. It isn't the best coffee around, but good enough."

The man in the gold jacket looked their way. Lee smiled and placed a hand on her shoulder. "I think he wants us to go."

Her eyes danced at his. "Then we'd better."

Chapter Thirty-Four

Lee left Elena in the parking lot with the idea they would meet up for dinner later that evening. He hitched a cab to First Street, to his condo in the city. He hadn't been there in years. He paid the driver, climbed the steps to the fourth floor, and walked down the red-carpeted hallway until he reached four-sixteen. He reached in his pocket and withdrew his keys. He placed the house key to the knob, but it wouldn't fit. He looked around and tried again. The door shot open and a hefty Italian-looking man glowered at him.

"Can I help you?"

Lee's eyes went wide. "I'm sorry, I must have the wrong place. My sister gave me the key. I thought she said four-sixteen. My mistake."

The man shut the door in Lee's face without another word.

A sense of helplessness flooded him. He didn't know where he worked or lived. Another man he didn't know occupied his home, and his job was now Don's. Am I still rich? He had to be. His body still existed in the pricy hospital and he had money in his wallet.

He walked back outside and down the street to a small park. He spotted an empty park bench in the middle, sat, and inspected the late afternoon sky. Forbearing clouds drifted overhead, blocking the sun. He pulled his coat close around him and sighed. If it rained, he'd be sunk. He had a date with Elena later, and without knowledge of where to change, he would show up soaked.

He stretched out his legs in front of him and watched a dog run down the grassy knoll in the distance to fetch a ball. A young girl collected dandelions from the grass while a mother watched from nearby. Several businessmen rushed past blocking his view, oblivious to the man on the bench. The contrast made him consider his lifestyle. Before his coma, he never just sat down and thought about things. His life was about making money—rushing past the destitute and exploiting the vulnerable. Elena was right. I am a monster. He almost wished he could regain his amnesia. Reality hurt. God why am I here?

"Freddy?"

Lee looked up.

A woman with gray hair sat on the grass reading a book a few feet away. "Is that you?"

He stared at her.

Did he know her?

She pushed up with a cane and came to his side.

"Aunt Tori?"

Her eyes glistened. She put out her arms, and they embraced. His body shook. It had been so long. "I'm so sorry," he said.

She pulled back and wiped the tears from his face with her soft hands. "Shh...no, don't apologize." She kissed his cheek and motioned for him to sit back down. "Boy, how I've missed you. You're all grown up now." Her salt-and-pepper hair, wrinkles, and age spots were evidence of their time apart. While he was gone, she aged. He did the math in his head. She must be almost seventy.

"How did you know it was me?"

"I saw your name in the paper." She grabbed his hand and squeezed. "I thought you were dead."

Lee laughed. "Yeah, seems to be the popular thing to say to me these days."

She wrapped her arm around the back of the bench and touched his shoulder. "What happened to you?"

He looked down the sidewalk and shrugged. "I ran away and started working at a firm called Melton and Gray. I started in the mailroom."

She seemed surprised. "You work in a mailroom?"

"I did. I got promoted and..." Lee stopped. What story should he tell her? He didn't have a clue who he was anymore. "What about you? Did you marry that Bobby guy?"

"No, Robert and I broke up a long time ago." She looked down at her hands. "I didn't do so well after you left."

A queasy feeling swept through his stomach. "Are you okay now?"

She glanced at him with a half-grin. "I will be." She sighed. "Come on. How about you help your old aunt home and let her make you some soup?"

"I'd love some soup." He stood and offered his arm.

She took it and they walked down the sidewalk to the street corner. A light drizzle blanketed the air. While waiting for the crosswalk, Lee closed his eyes and breathed in the rain. The wet asphalt smelled like burning tar, but it comforted him. The last time he stopped to experience a new rain he was probably a kid.

A green hand flashed on the box in front of them and they crossed to the other side. "Where do you live?" he asked.

She pointed to a brown apartment complex about a block down the road.

"You sold the house?"

"A few years ago." She squeezed up against him. "That big house was too much to keep up. This place was quainter and suited me."

They walked up a small flight of stairs and down a yellow corridor. At the second from the last door, she stopped at a blue door. He couldn't believe it. "You still have a blue door?"

She grinned and unlocked the knob. "I made such a stink and the landlord likes me. He finally gave in."

Inside, the décor resembled the house he lived in decades ago. The same brown curtains hung on the windows and an old clay pot from his fifth-grade art class decorated the mantle. A cream, flowered couch sat in the middle of the tiny room, next to a small glass end table.

She dropped her coat, purse, and keys on a small stool by the door. "Can I get you anything to drink?"

"Ice water would be wonderful."

She turned for the kitchen, and Lee followed her in. The room consisted of all the regular kitchen appliances, but all within feet of one another. Without moving from one spot, she managed to grab a cup, fill it with ice and water, hand it to him, and then grab a pot from the cabinet.

"How about rock soup?"

Lee grinned. "I love that story."

"It's a soup, not a book, dear." She winked. "But it

did help me get you to eat vegetables when you were a kid. Before that, you wouldn't eat anything except pizza or frozen nuggets."

"I only ate the soup to find the rock." He took a sip from his glass of water. The ice clanked on the side of the cup and a memory of his class project came back to him. They had read the book Rock Soup in class. The teacher thought it would be fun if everyone were to bring in his or her favorite vegetable to put in the soup. He hated vegetables, so the teacher assigned him to bring the rock—a pinto bean that hadn't been soaked. The kid who found the rock won a prize. Lee didn't find it, but it was fun trying. After that, his aunt had to make him rock soup every weekend.

"Rock soup it is," he said.

His aunt filled a pot with water, placed it on the stove, and turned the burner to high. She opened the refrigerator and pulled out some cooked chicken in a plastic baggy and dumped it in the pot. She then squatted and pulled celery, carrots, an onion, mushrooms, and some garlic from the crisper. "Would you mind chopping some carrots and celery?"

He reached out his hand. "Anything but the onion."

She laughed and placed the vegetables on the counter. "Here." She handed him a plastic cutting board and then pointed to his right. "There's a knife in the drawer behind you."

Lee turned and pulled out a paring knife. He withdrew a few carrots from the plastic bag and washed them in the sink. He then repeated the process with the celery. "So, Auntie, why are you so down? I can't remember ever seeing you so sad."

She pulled the skin off the garlic and dropped a few bulbs in the water. "There is no easy way to reveal this, so I'm going to just say it." She tossed what was left of the garlic in the trash by her foot and turned to face him. "I have cancer, Freddy."

Lee stopped chopping. "What?"

"I found out about a year ago. I tried to find you." She touched his cheek with the back of her hand. "No one wants to die alone."

He knew what that felt like. Tears pushed at the corners of his eyes. He set the knife down and pulled her to him.

She wrapped her arms around his waist and held him close. Together, they cried. Tears of sorrow, sadness, regret, and joy.

God, I don't want her to die alone.

She pulled away and wiped her eyes with a paper towel. "Thanks for being here, Freddy. How I've missed you, boy."

"Yeah, me too."

"Okay, we've got work to do. How are the carrots and celery coming?"

"Was chopping the last stock before you started blubbering." He smiled playfully.

She returned his smile and reached for the cutting board. "Still have a smart mouth, huh?" She placed the board over the stove and the vegetables sprinkled into the pot like rain. "What kind of noodles do you want?"

"Macaroni, if you have them."

"I do." She reached into a cabinet over her head and pulled down a brown box. "But I hope you can tolerate wheat pasta. The doctor has me eating less sugar and carbs."

Compassion for his ill aunt invaded his heart. He felt choked up. "Can I use your bathroom?"

"Sure, hon. Just go down the hall to your left." She motioned with her free hand. "Can't miss it. It's the one without a bed."

He tried to smile, before running from the room. His throat hurt, his eyes burned. A forklift of remorse had just been dumped on his conscience, and it stung. Opening the door, he turned on the light. A vintage claw-foot tub sat on the left and a sink and toilet to his right. He flipped on the sink faucet and splashed water on his face. How did he remove the weight on his chest? He'd never felt like this. Wait, once. The day his mother had died. He felt responsible for her need to make life-altering decisions—decisions that led to her death. Yes, he felt like this then. He spent his entire life running from the feeling and now he had just slammed into the same wall.

There was a light rap at the door. "Freddy, are you okay?"

He looked at his reflection. Water dripped down his face, his eyes were red, his complexion pallid. He took a deep breath and lied. "Yeah, I'm fine. I'll be out in a moment."

"The soup should be done in a few minutes. It never takes long once the water boils."

"Okay." Lee reached for a soft beige towel and patted his face dry. He had to pull himself together in order to enjoy his day. He rolled his shoulders back and lifted his chin. Big breath in. Time to eat rock soup.

In the dining room, steam lazed above the bowls on the table. "What would you like to drink?" his aunt asked, placing two cups on the table.

"Do you have any soda?"

"Only diet." She grinned. "Less sugar. I could also make ice tea."

"Sugar-free is fine. I acquired a taste for it when my wife went on a diet."

She flipped around. "Wife?"

Oh no. *"Yeah, um, Elena Snow." How could he explain they weren't married yet, but they had spent the last twenty years together as man and wife? "Actually, we've been separated, but are working on getting back together."*

"Well, if there is a Mrs. Avarice, I would like to meet her."

Lee sat at the table and inhaled the rich chicken broth. It took him back. "You will, in time." Once he fixed things.

"Great, now that that's settled, eat. It's only good when it's hot."

He dipped the spoon in the clear liquid and brought it to his mouth. One sip and he knew why rock soup had always been his favorite. "Delicious, Auntie."

"Thank you." She sat next to him and sprinkled some hot pepper in hers. "Not supposed to have these either, but what is life without a few moments of impetuousness."

After enjoying three helpings, Lee realized it was time to pick up Elena. They were supposed to go to a new steak house in Coronado, but at the moment, food was far from his mind. "Thank you for everything. It was so good to see you."

"Can you give me your number?"

Lee looked at his hands and then met her eyes. "I'm kind of between places right now, but as soon as I have a phone, I'll call you with it."

She lifted his chin between her fingers and squeezed. "Don't you dare disappear on me again."

He tried to smile, but probably just looked like a "chubby bunny." He slurred through his pinched cheeks. "I walt Antae, I promase."

She kissed him hard on the forehead and grinned. "I love you, son."

His eyes glazed over again and he pulled her into a hug. "I love you too, Aunt Tori." He stepped back. "And thanks for lunch."

"Any time."

****

Stan checked his watch and entered the café in a rush. Instantly, he knew he was in trouble. Kari's head was buried in her hands. This would be the sixth or seventh time he'd left her waiting for him.

She looked up and offered pinched smile.

"Hi." His kissed her cheek. "Sorry, I'm late."

She shrugged. "You missed the wedding planner."

His stomach flipped. "Sorry. Did you two figure stuff out?"

She pushed a wedding magazine to the side and leaned in. "Um, all but a date."

"A date?"

"When we're getting married."

He stared at her, unable to speak. Luckily, he didn't have to. His cell rang.

"Heller." He listened to an order to return to the office with relief. "Right away, sir." He hung up and forced a grin. "We'll have to talk about this later. I have another lead on the case. Call me later?"

She nodded.

"Great." He stood and kissed her. "Bye."

****

"You didn't eat much," Elena said, looking down at Lee's half-eaten steak.

"I had a big lunch with my aunt this afternoon. I guess I wasn't that hungry." Lee folded his napkin over his plate and pushed it away. "You want to take a walk on the beach?"

"I'd love to."

He pulled his wallet out of his pocket and flipped it open. He was glad to see there were several credit cards inside. He grabbed the top one and tossed it on the bill.

The waitress took the leather folder and disappeared.

"How long have you lived in San Diego?" Elena asked.

He had to think about that. What part of his life was he currently in? "Since I was ten. You?"

He knew the answer.

"Two years. I'm originally from the Buena Park area up by Hollywood, but right now I'm taking classes at San Diego State."

"What in?"

She toyed with an empty straw wrapper on the table. "Humanities. I bet you don't know what that is. Most people don't."

He smiled. "Actually, I do. It's a foo-foo degree."

She laughed.

How he had missed her laugh.

"Foo-foo huh?"

He winked.

"For the record, Humanities is not a foo-foo

degree. It's actually pretty deep. It is the expression of self. It is art, literature, theatre, music, philosophy, and history. It's life through illustration, thought, creativity, and meaning. There really is nothing foo-foo about it."

Lee grew serious. "There's nothing foo-foo about you either. You're amazing."

She stared at him. Her expression filled with joy. Years of marriage had taught him, solace to Elena meant elation.

The waitress returned with his card. He signed the top receipt, grabbed the bottom one, and stuffed it in his pocket. "Come on. Let's go."

The restaurant sat just steps away from the beach. Lee and Elena removed their shoes and stepped out on the sand. The supple earth mingled between their toes. The waves crashed in the darkness and the brisk air smelled of salt and fish. Amber streetlights about every ten feet lit their path.

Elena squeezed her hands against her shoulders.

"Are you cold?"

She shook her head. "No, I'm okay. I love it down here." She looped her arm in his. "But if you're looking for a reason to wrap your arm around me, you don't need one."

Lee stopped and faced her. Her features looked angelic in the soft light. He touched her chin and brought his lip to hers. She responded and wrapped her arms around his neck. As, they kissed in the darkness, his heart hammered. You have a second chance. Don't blow it.

Chapter Thirty- Five

Stan sipped from the milk carton in his hand. The cafeteria was vacant except for a doctor, a custodian, and Kari. He set the carton down and smiled. "When do you get off work?"

"Not for another five hours." She pushed cherries from her half-eaten pie around her plate, mixing them with the crust. "What's funny is I used to live for the graveyard shift." She reached out and interlaced her fingers through his. "But now that I have you, I don't really want to be here."

"I feel the same. Once I wrap this case, we'll set a date. I promise."

She withdrew her hand. Her face soured. "And when will that be?"

He shrugged and stabbed a piece of brownie on his plate. "It shouldn't take forever."

"Yeah? I've heard some cases can take years and some become cold." She sighed. "I don't want to be a seventy-year old maid, waiting for you to solve this crime."

"I won't wait that long."

Her eyes narrowed.

He reached for her hand again. "I'm still grieving, Kari. This is part of that process. If I'm not able to solve it in a few months, we'll set a date anyway."

"Why not just set it now and see?" She squeezed

his hand.

His gaze dropped to his crumb-filled plate. What could he say? There wasn't an ounce of uncertainty he wanted to marry her. That wasn't the issue at all. It was the fact he couldn't be happy without resolution. "Just give me a little more time, okay?"

She shoved her plate away and leaned to grab her purse. "I should get back."

"Kari, please don't be angry."

She half-grinned, pushed back her chair, and stood. "I'm not mad. I'll see you tomorrow." With that, she walked down the hall and disappeared into the elevator.

Stan wanted to run after her and tell her he was sorry. That life wasn't fair. He wished they'd met before he was so messed up. Maybe then they would have been happy. He piled the plates on a tray and walked them to the kitchen window, where a Hispanic man reached out and took the tray.

Stan grabbed his coat from the back of the chair just as the cell phone rang inside his pocket. He dug it out and flipped it open. "Hello?"

"Heller, where are you?" the captain barked. "I've been trying you on the radio for ten minutes."

"Sorry, sir. I stopped for dinner."

"Well, finish up and get down to Sunset Pier. There's been a stabbing."

Stan walked to the outside door and pushed on the bar. The brisk night air nipped at his cheeks. "I'm on my way. Should be there in fifteen minutes."

"Good." The captain hung up.

Stan stuffed the phone back in his pocket. Good was right. Work would keep his mind off things. He jumped in his Jeep, started the engine, and caught the first freeway entrance toward Sunset.

****

Fred looked from the mirror to Bill lying on the floor next to the bed. The old man didn't look well. His face seemed paler than usual, almost gray, and the cockeyed way he was holding his head made him seem feeble. "Hey, you okay?"

Bill looked up through cracked lids. "Must have been something I ate."

"You're a spirit. You don't eat."

"Maybe that's the problem." Bill smirked. "How about fixing me some pork chops and applesauce. Easy on the mint."

Fred took a seat next to him. "You'd go to your grave making jokes, wouldn't you?"

"Who says I'm not already there?"

Fred patted his companion's thigh. "You never did tell me who you are. Are you a ghost or something?"

"Ha! So, you are Fred's imagination after all. Because that was a good one."

"Yeah, I suppose." He didn't know what to do with the emotion he felt for his companion. Sympathy was a feeling he had denied himself since his mom died. It was a sentiment divergent to his profession. If he allowed his compassion to get in the way, he would never have made it big at Melton and Gray. But he wasn't that man anymore. The truth was he couldn't deny how seeing Bill made him feel. His heart ached. Just like when he saw his aunt. He let go of the wall again—and the dam broke. Years of pain, regret, and mourning piled onto him. Though it wasn't pleasant, it felt good to feel. Tears slid down his cheeks in a wave of emotion.

"Well, now I've seen all. None of the coma dupes before shed buckets."

Fred wiped his eyes with the back of his sleeve and looked away. "I'm just thinking about my aunt."

Bill patted Fred's leg. "You keep telling yourself that. In the meantime, I think you're doing well."

"My life is fading away. Everything I know doesn't exist anymore. I am pretty lost."

Bill pushed up on his elbows and grinned. "You were already fading away, but now you have a chance to live for once, to grow, and find true happiness. Being rich, as you now know, doesn't ensure success and happiness." The door opened and he looked up. "You must have fixed something, because your Mrs. has returned."

Fred spun around. *Elena.* He exhaled. She was back.

She rolled the stool over to the side of the bed and grabbed his hand. Tears trickled to the white blanket. "Oh, honey, come back to me. I need you."

"Excuse me, Mrs. Avarice?" Stan stood in the doorway. "I'm sorry to disturb you. I'm Detective Heller, and I'm trying to find the person responsible for this. I wondered if I could ask you a few questions?"

She dabbed at her eyes and sniffed. "Yeah, sure. Come on in."

He flipped the switch on the wall and moved to the chair at the end of the bed. "I believe we spoke on the phone a while back."

"I recognize you from the newspaper."

He frowned. "Yeah, not one of my better days. My father meant a lot to me."

She nodded, looking down at the hand she held.

"Yeah, and if what I've read is accurate, your father died investigating the mess surrounding my husband's company." She once again met Stan's gaze. "I'm sorry about that, but I'd like to help."

"Yeah." He sighed. "Do you know what might have caused your husband to be shot in the first place?"

She seemed to ponder that before answering. "Well, he didn't have too many friends, and he worked with wealthy and powerful people. One enemy in particular was Asher Melton of Melton and Gray. Guess Lee did something to upset him years ago. Hasn't trusted him since."

He scribbled some notes on a pad. "Does the name Scott Mueller mean anything to you?"

She nodded. "Yes, he worked for my mother. Maybe even dated her for a while."

"We found him shot in the Snow Building a few days ago. We believe there is a connection between his shooting and the tycoon serial killer."

Color drained from her face. "My mother? Is she okay?"

Stan sighed. "As far as we know. She wasn't there. The authorities are trying to find her for questioning."

"But you don't think she did it?" Tears formed in her eyes, ready to spill.

"Honestly, we don't know what to think. We have to follow all leads."

"I always assumed it was Asher." She toyed with her wedding ring. "He was such an intimidating man. Huge and manipulative. He hated my husband. But from what I've heard, he's one of the victims."

"We have evidence that suggests Asher Melton was the last person to see your husband alive. That doesn't indicate he pulled the trigger, but it may be a sign he knew something." Stan pinched his lips together in a defeated smile. "As you already pointed out, he's not a breathing witness."

Fred stood and paced. He was sure Melton shot him. *If not my boss, who?*

"The tycoon murders all had Melton in common, right?" Elena asked.

Stan glanced at her. "Yeah."

"Could it be Asher was killed for revenge or maybe even self-defense?"

He scratched his chin with the eraser of his pencil. "I thought about that, but the evidence suggests that all the murders, including his own, happened in the same manner and with the same gun. Whoever shot Melton was more than just some vengeful person who knew how to throw us off. This murder and all the others were planned."

Elena reached for her husband's hand again and brought it to her lips. She kissed his knuckles and then laid it back down. Her love for the man lying on the bed touched Fred's heart. He, of course, was that man, but he wasn't worthy of it. No, the man in the bed deserved to be where he was. Fred knew that. He wished he could undo all he had done, so that he actually earned her love.

"And Clayton Gray?"

"Suicide."

She shook her head. "I only met him once. He was a lot different than Asher. I sensed he was the puppet master, pulling the strings, but stayed away from the dirt."

"Yes, his investment was a financial one. He left

Mr. Melton to do the dirty work." Stan glanced at his notes. "I have to ask. How did your mom feel about your marriage?"

Elena walked to the window and lifted the blinds. "She was angry enough to have him killed."

"Really?"

"Maybe. I don't know. She sought to control me anyway she could. If it could be bought, she would pay the price. Including men." She turned back. "But I don't think she is capable of murder."

"I hope you're right." Stan stood and held out his hand. "Well, I'll leave you alone now. Thank you for your time."

Elena shook it. "Thank you, Detective. I really appreciated you calling me to pray the other day." She paused. "I know your family sacrificed a lot."

He nodded and left.

She returned to the body and traced his face with the back of her hand. "Well, Lee, I should get home. Laura can only watch Becky for an hour." She leaned in and kissed his lips. "I love you, darling. You come home soon, okay?"

"Did she just imply I have a kid?" Fred asked.

Bill lifted his left eyebrow. "You didn't before?"

"No. The business demanded all of my time."

"And your heart."

"Yeah, okay, and my heart."

"You need a cigar." Bill popped him on the back and handed him a pink bubblegum stick. "Congrats, Daddy-o."

Fred stared at the fake cigar. "Where'd you get that?"

Bill shook his head. "The boy never learns.

Imagination, my friend. Imagination. Yours to be exact."

"So, will I wake up someday and realize this mirror thing and my time with you has all a ruse? My mind's eye playing tricks on me?" He looked over at his wife. "Will she have really left me? Will I have no chance at being a father?"

Bill ran a hand over his balding head. "I don't know."

"How can you not know? Aren't you the all-powerful spirit guide? Don't you know if this is a dream or reality?"

"No, because if I could answer that, then I'd know who I am."

What?

Elena opened the door, glanced over her shoulder, and blew the body a kiss. "I'll come by and see you tomorrow. Be good." And she left.

Could I really be a father? They must have named her Becky after his mom, Rebecca. He needed to go back in time just to see his child born. If he did have a child, then he had to thrust through and find the answer to getting better. A surge of hope sprang into his heart. Could there be life beyond this coma? Even if it were a dream, he would enjoy the vacation.

He pushed himself up. "I need to go back in and make a modification that will get me out of this bed."

"Who's to say this isn't God's will and that you won't end up in a coma no matter what you do?"

Fred glared at him. "What are you saying, old man? That I'm doomed to live the rest of my life in this bed?"

Bill shrugged. "Bright and dark lights, *young*

man."

"Don't start that again."

"This coma was a blessing. Admit it."

"I don't deny it, but I also know that *if* I have the power to change my destiny, then I need to take it. Wouldn't you agree? You're the one who taught me that."

Bill laid the back of his head on the tile and stared at the ceiling. His face was sallow, his eyes glassy and withdrawn.

Fred squatted next him. "What's happening to you, Bill? Can you die? I mean, are you able to?"

"My job is almost done here. I will go onto my next task once this one's completed." Bill closed his eyes, crossed his hands over his chest, and relaxed.

"Very funny. Don't you dare leave me."

Bill didn't move.

"Bill?" Fred nudged him, but he still didn't move. "Wake up, please." Tears welled in his eyes. "I'm not ready for you to go yet."

The old man peeked through one lid and smiled. "I didn't know you cared."

Fred smacked his arm and stood. "That's the cruelest joke yet. And you think *I* need a heart transplant." He walked to the mirror, not wanting to look back at his companion. He knew Bill wasn't joking this time. The old man might be making light of how he felt, but he couldn't hide the truth. His time with Fred was short.

****

Stan typed the last bit of information on the screen and pressed print. Next to him, the machine buzzed to life and spit out his report. Now he could go home. He grabbed the paper, shoved it in a manila sleeve, and stood. Files flowed from the captain's box. Stan tossed his into the mix and turned to go.

"You out of here?" Bogan called behind him.

Stan turned.

She wore a form-fitting black suit and pearls.

"You look very professional, Officer Bogan. Guess you're not picking up tricks on El Cajon Boulevard tonight, huh?"

She rolled her eyes. "I'm here to give you the details on the hair sample we found in the Snow office."

He stepped forward like a dog waiting for crumbs. "Do we have a suspect?"

Bogan looked away, holding a red file pinched between her thumb and index finger.

"Who?" Stan snatched the folder from her hand. "Tell me it wasn't the mother-in-law." He flipped it open and scanned the page. The hairs on the back of his neck stood up and his body tingled. The room seemed to sway. He rested against the desk behind him. "This can't be right."

She moved next to him and placed her hand on his shoulder. "I'm sorry, but it was conclusive. Finger prints and other DNA in the room confirmed it."

As Stan slipped the file under his arm, adrenaline surged through his body. He vaulted out the station entrance, racing to his car. *Here we go.*

Chapter Thirty-Six

Lee stood in the delivery room next to Elena, holding her hand. Sweat and agony covered her face, but a smile still broke through.

"Push again," the doctor said at the foot of the bed. "You're almost there."

Elena grimaced and squeezed Lee's hand. A scream reverberated from her chest.

"You can do it, sweetheart," Lee whispered.

She shot him a look that said, not another word. He tried to smile back.

The doctor peered over the sheet. "The baby's head is out now. Just a few more pushes, Elena, to clear the shoulders."

She tried a few more times, and finally, the baby's cry coursed in the air. Lee stared at the small child with awe.

The nurse offered him a pair of scissors. "Would you like to cut the cord?"

He nodded and stepped forward. His hand shook as he clamped the metal edge down. The cord severed, and the doctor laid the baby on Elena's stomach. Lee felt dizzy with delight. He had a daughter. He looked back at his wife. She appeared exhausted, but happy. Lee had never known such joy. If this was indeed a dream, he didn't want to wake up.

****

"Bill, you're never going to believe how beautiful my baby girl is." Fred turned from the mirror. "She looks just like my wife. A full head of black hair. Did you see her? Did you?" He stopped. Something was wrong. "Bill?"

"Shh!" Bill hissed from behind the curtain.

Fred knelt next to him and whispered, "What?"

Bill pointed to the bed.

A woman stood in the dark shadows of the room, staring at the body. Something shiny hung in her hand.

"Who is she?"

Bill shook his head. "I think she may be the one who shot you."

Fred looked back at her. "No, I told you. Melton shot me. That's what I remember."

"Well, she doesn't think he did a good enough job, because she's been brandishing that weapon at your skull for quite some time. I was worried you wouldn't make it back before…"

"Before what?"

Bill pinched his lips together and peered up at Fred with a grave look.

Fred flinched. "You don't think she's going to shoot me?"

"Yes, I do. And you better start praying, because your life is as good as last week's Chinese food."

Panic seeped through his pores. "What do I do? I'm a dead man. How can I fix this?"

"I don't think you can. You didn't figure out what to change, so here you are. Ready to meet the Creator of the Universe. Say hi for me, okay?" Bill sighed.

The woman whispered in the body's ear. "Have you figured it out yet? Do you remember me, Freddy?"

"She called me Freddy. Not Lee."

"So?"

"So, that means she knew me before I left my aunt's house."

"You may not remember me." She stuck out her tongue and ran it up his cheek. "But boy do I remember you."

"Okay, she's demented." Bill cringed. "She just took a taste test of your sweaty face."

Fred realized his mouth was open and snapped it shut. *Who is she?* He couldn't get a clear look at her in the blackness, but her voice sounded vaguely familiar.

She curled her arm around the crown of his head and leaned in. "Oh, how you made my life miserable. I only wish I could have seen you suffer a bit more." She squeezed his temples and leaned back. "You got off way too easy. Sleeping in this cushy bed for over a year is nothing." She flicked his face with her nails. "Where's the torture in that?" She hopped up on the bed and straddled his chest. "When I told Asher I was going to kill you, he was afraid I'd go to jail. So, he went to do it for me. He thought he was doing me a favor, but he was wrong." She ran the barrel of her gun down his arm. "I wanted the chance to shoot my biggest enemy myself. When I found out you were still alive, I was disappointed. Now I'll have my revenge."

"Bill." Fred's voice wavered. "She's going to kill me."

"Pray, my friend." Bill knelt to the floor and clasped his hands in front of him. "Pray!"

Fred stared motionless, stunned.

The door shot open and Stan snapped on the lights. Fred looked from the detective to the woman on his bed. He knew her. It was Krystal, Melton's girlfriend. She rolled off the bed and faced the detective with arms folded.

"Krissy?"

"Hurray! The cavalry's arrived!" Bill yelled.

She shoved the gun under the pillow and smiled. "Stan." She ran and embraced him. "How are you, big brother?"

He unwrapped from her arms and pushed her back. "What are you doing here?"

"You haven't seen me in years, and that's the best you can do?"

He didn't look amused. "Just answer the question."

"I'm visiting an old friend. What's it to you?" She backed up to the bed and placed her hand by the pillow. "I should ask you what you're doing here. Are you still a cop? Abiding in good old Dad's dream."

"Yeah, I'm still a cop." He stepped to the end of the bed, hand on hip, expression cold. "I'm curious to know what you've been up to for the past couple years."

Something moved next to Fred's leg, and he jumped. "Bill, move over."

Bill pushed against him, smiling. "Sorry, this is going to get good. Wish we had some popcorn."

"Use your imagination," Fred said dryly.

"Who knew the man was brilliant?" Bill snapped his fingers and a red and white tub filled with popped *kernels* appeared in his lap. "Hope you like butter. I imagined a lot."

"Oh, you know, bro, just living it up with the rich and famous. Doing what I do best." Krystal pushed a lock of her blonde hair over her ear. "Conning people out of his or her millions. Isn't that what you'd expect from me?"

Stan sat on the back of the chair, with his legs resting on the seat. "No, I would like to think you turned out okay. You're a smart girl. Dad and I both prayed that—"

"Stop! Please." She glared at him. "Who was it that told me, almost every day, I was a big loser? Our father, that's who. You were his golden child." A tear made a path in her makeup. "You were his prized son, the one who would follow in his footsteps. But not me." She sniffed. "No, not me. I was the family disappointment. The one who stole his priceless family heirloom out of his drawer at age fifteen. He never got over that." Her voice lowered almost to a whisper. "He never trusted me again."

"That's not true."

She hit him with a defiant stare. "That's why I left the moment I turned eighteen. I was so sick of feeling worthless. Beneath the Heller family name."

"That was over twenty years ago. You can't blame your troubles on something that happened to you in high school."

She stuck her tongue in her cheek and snarled. "Oh yeah, that's easy for you to say. That one moment changed me into an undesirable person in the Heller home."

He stepped forward. "But what does this have to do with Lee Avarice?"

"Yeah," Fred said.

The light flickered in the hallway. Krystal glanced around the room, her eyes locking on the bedridden body. Her voice was hoarse, her face red and swollen.

"Freddy took away my childhood."

Fred stepped forward.

"And how did he do that?" Stan asked.

Her eyes narrowed. "It was because of him I stole that ring."

"What?" Fred said.

Stan glanced at the body. "Who is he to you?"

"He was a guy at school who fooled me with some trick dice."

"Oh no." Fred squeezed his eyes closed, adrenaline making him dizzy.

She glared at the man on the bed. "He threatened to have his friend beat me up if I didn't pay, and I believed him." She sat on the stool and blotted her face with her hand. "I was too scared to tell Dad I had gambled, so I didn't. I took Grandma's ring out of his sock drawer while he was bowling."

Fred couldn't believe it. Now he knew. All his troubles had started in high school.

Stan shook his head, an expression of disbelief apparent on his face. "So, you shot him?"

"Not yet." She slid her hand under the pillow, pulled out the gun, and brought it to the body's temple.

Stan jumped off the chair, hands up in mock surrender. "Whoa! Don't do this."

"Asher didn't want me to shoot him the first time. He was always trying to save me, but he didn't realize I was not redeemable."

"That's not true, Krystal. You don't want to do this. Come on, put the gun down. You'll go to jail for murder."

She laughed through her tears. "No. I came here to finish the job." She wiped her eyes on her sleeve. "Jail for murder? Ha! You think I can't do this?" The barrel lifted to face her brother. "I've killed eleven men in the past year, and you don't think I can't do this one. He's the whole reason they were all shot."

A guttural noise shot out of Stan's throat. "You killed Dad?"

"Don't be absurd. Asher shot Dad."

"Asher Melton?" Stan looked at her, his face drained of color. "Explain."

"I ran into Lee in the mailroom one day. It took me a while, but eventually, I placed him as the boy I knew in high school. My bitterness and anger just got worse and worse. And I was out of control." She flipped her hair. "Asher demanded to know what was going on. I told him my story...that he stole from me and basically ruined my life." She leaned against the wall, staring at the body. "Asher said he'd take care of it. But I wanted to fight my own battle. Dad discovered my part in this and came to arrest me. Asher intervened." She sniffed. "He shot Dad."

Perspiration beaded on Stan's forehead. "And the tycoon murders?"

"Asher should not have killed Dad. I despised him, yes, but he was still my father." Her face turned rigid, her eyes void of light. "The murders were in a sense revenge for killing Dad."

Stan's face went ash. He looked like he might vomit. "Why not just kill Melton? Why kill all his executives?"

She shrugged. "The first one was to throw the cops off my trail, the second..." A mordant grin played on her lips. "Revenge. Each time, Asher would come home broken. It was exhilarating. I never felt so alive—so in control."

Stan's face contorted. "You're not well."

The gun moved in his direction, her hand shaking, lips quivering. "Don't say that about me, Stan. I'm not who you and Dad thought I was."

"You're worse," he rasped.

Her chest seemed to heave and she cleared her throat to talk. "You made and destroyed me. I was a good girl."

Stan laughed. "Yeah, I'm sure all serial killers say that."

She let out an ear-piercing shriek.

The detective grabbed his ears. "Krissy, stop! We can work this out."

The two coma companions also clutched the sides of their head.

"Boy, that woman needs a good, old-fashioned spanking," Bill yelled.

"Please! You want security to come in here?" Stan asked.

She ceased and glared at him.

"No," Fred said. "Keep screaming, let them come. Let them come."

"He's trying to handle this," Bill said.

"Now he's going to pay." She leveled the gun at the body's head.

"Well, he's not doing a good job," Fred said.

She pressed the barrel into the body's temple. "After this, I don't care what happens to me."

"She's really going to shoot me!"

"No, Krissy," Stan shouted. "Don't do it!"

"But I know how to stop her," Fred said.

She cocked the gun.

Bill pushed Fred to the mirror. "Hurry!"

"Say good-bye, Freddy."

****

The sound of Sam's locker door slammed closed.

Fred jumped, startled. "You scared me, buddy."

"Sorry." Sam snapped his lock closed. "You got the die with you?"

Fred reached into his pocket and felt the two plastic cubes. "Yeah, I've got them."

Sam tossed his backpack over his left shoulder. "Well come on then. I've got the perfect pigeon. Krissy Heller is willing to bet she can beat you, but you always win." He tugged Fred's jacket and waved for him to follow. "She's in the quad."

Fred stepped over wet socks and soiled gym shorts to get to the door. The room smelled of sweat and mildew, a flashback he'd gladly forget.

They shot through the double doors and sauntered to the open lunch area. Teenagers sporting feathered hair, sweater vests, and zipper pants sat cross-legged on the grass eating from sack lunches. Fred tried not to laugh. Could he have really looked so ridiculous?

On the other side of the fountain, he spotted her. She waved them over.

"Hi, Krissy," Fred said as he sat on the cement wall.

She blew a bubble, skimmed the courtyard, and sucked her gum back in. "Did you bring some dice?"

Fred looked at Sam and then back to Krissy. He already knew the response he'd get. But he wasn't really in high school anymore. He didn't have to be popular. He just wanted to live, to have a life with his wife and new baby girl.

"Krissy, can I talk to you alone for a moment?"

Sam raised an eyebrow. "What gives, Freddy? We going to do this or not?"

Fred patted his shoulder. "Trust me, okay?"

Sam sighed, nodded, and walked to the picnic tables by the cafeteria.

Freddy turned back to Krissy and grinned. "I can't take your money."

"You won't. I'll win." She swung her hand in the air, knocking a potato chip bag from her lap onto the blacktop.

Fred reached over and retrieved it. "Look, I like you, so I can't do it."

Her mouth hung open as she leaned toward him. "You like me, like me."

He grinned. "Yeah, but Sam likes you more. So, I can't make a move just yet."

She stared at him for a moment. "They're trick die, huh?"

Fred bit the side of his cheek and glanced at Sam standing a few yards away, watching them. "Yeah. They are."

"Can I see them?" She put out her hand, which was covered in henna art.

"I like your tattoos. Did you do them yourself?"

She turned her wrist over, revealing more. "Yeah, some of it. Brooke helped me with the rest."

Fred pulled the die from his pocket. He lifted her decorated wrist and twisted it lightly so her palm faced him again. "Here." He laid the die in her hand and gazed into her eyes.

She rolled them a few times. "Can I trick someone?"

Fred thought about that for a moment. No, he couldn't let her take another dishonest route. He was here to change her direction in life. To make her okay. "I said I like you." Fred kissed her hard on the mouth. When he pulled away, her eyes fluttered open and a slow grin crossed her face. The die rolled out of her hand and onto the stone wall.

"What about Sam?" She sounded winded.

Fred scooped up the die and placed them back in his pocket. He glanced over at his friend, who had a look of bewilderment plastered on his face. "I wouldn't want to do anything to hurt his feelings. Maybe the three of us could go to the winter dance together?"

She glanced at the redheaded boy waiting for them and smiled. "I'd like that."

Chapter Thirty- Seven

Fred blinked. "Bill, I think I did it. I think I really did it." He paused and looked around. He stood in an enormous bathroom. "Where am I? Bill?" He walked out the door and stopped in surprise. He was in his master suite back home. A woman slept on the bed in front of him. He tiptoed to the bed and pulled back the covers. Relief escaped his lips. It was Elena.

He took in the room and then hurried back into the restroom to look in the mirror again. A carbon copy stared back at him. He rubbed his hand across the silver pane. So, I'm no longer Dracula. He brought his hand to the spot where Melton's bullet had gone through his head. It was solid. Never touched. It never happened.

Is this a dream? He pinched his arm and reveled in the pain that followed. He ran his hands over his body, patting his chest, his legs, and his neck. I'm really here, alive, and in my body. He buckled to the floor, sobbing, overwhelmed by it all.

When he pulled himself together, he walked back to his bed and climbed between the covers. He wrapped his arm over his wife, and she squirmed to face him. "I love you," he whispered in her ear.

She mumbled, "I love you, too."

He kissed her cheek, pulled her close, and smiled.
Suddenly his eyes shot open. He was back in the

hospital room. It wasn't over.

"Krissy, put the gun down. You don't want to do this!" Stan yelled.

She cocked the trigger and a gun sounded. Her mouth dropped open in shock. Blood oozed out the hole on her left shoulder.

Stan stood feet away holding a smoking gun, tears streaming down his face. Within seconds, security burst through the door.

"Drop your weapon, sir."

Krystal folded to the floor.

Stan held his hands in the air. "I'm a cop."

"Drop your weapons, sir," a security guard said, holding him tight in the sight of his gun.

"I'm going to reach in my pocket and withdraw my badge," he said as he gently laid his gun to the floor.

"Slowly."

Stan reached in his pocket and slid the badge to the guard. He then rushed to his sister's side. Her labored breathing said she didn't have much time. "Get a doctor in here."

"Didn't you shoot her?"

"Hurry!"

The guard disappeared and Stan pulled her head into his lap. "I'm sorry we let you down, Krissy."

"I'm sorry, too," she gasped. Her eyes shut and her body relaxed.

****

A female voice sounded in the distance. "Good morning, Lee." His eyes felt like bricks. He pushed against the darkness. A faint outline of Nurse Kari blurred overhead. He tried to open his eyes. They burned.

"Oh my goodness! Are you waking up?" She studied him for a moment. Yes, you are. Welcome back, Mr. Avarice." She dropped his chart by his bed and hit a button on the wall. Her smile blossomed.

He wished he shared her enthusiasm. Last thing he remembered was being in bed with his wife. *What changed? Why am I in the hospital again?* He tried to lift his head, but it felt like a bowling ball. He labored to speak, but a tube stood in his way.

A doctor entered and peeked at the chart. He then busied himself checking Lee's vitals. After several tests, he reached for the breathing tube. "I think we can remove this."

The nurse and doctor removed the tube. It burned and gagged as it came out of his throat. Once free, he worked to speak, "Where am I?"

"You're in the Prospect Convalescent Hospital. You've been in a coma for quite a while. I'll let the doctor explain the rest when he gets here." She ran out of the room, giddy with delight.

Lee looked around, unaware of what was real and what wasn't. The room was similar to what he remembered, and yet different. Commotion sounded outside the door before a doctor, another nurse, and Kari ran in.

"Mr. Avarice, so glad to have you back. How do you feel?"

He blinked. "Like I've got a major hangover."

The doctor laughed. "I'll have to take your word on that. Never been a drinking man." He pulled a stethoscope from his neck, placed the tubes in his ears and the microphone on Lee's chest.

"Are you thirsty?" Kari grabbed a pink pitcher

from a table by the door.

Lee touched his tongue to the roof of his mouth a few times. It felt like he had swallowed wallpaper paste. He nodded and she poured him a glass. "Can I get you anything?"

His stomach rumbled. "I'd like to eat."

"That's a good sign," the doctor said. "Nurse Jensen. See what you can do."

She nodded and left.

The doctor straightened and grabbed a chart from the end of the bed. "Well, let's see what your brain has been doing for the past year."

****

Within hours of being awake, Lee grew restless. Too many doctors and nurses who had been in to poke and prod him. To them, he was a sick man who had just come out of a deep sleep. For him, he'd lived an amazing life of self-discovery and was now ready to make things right. What happened, or didn't happen, was still unclear. Elena hadn't been by, so he assumed the worst. He wanted answers, and he wanted a second chance. "Do you think I could visit the hospital chapel?"

The doctor tapped Lee's knee, and his foot jumped. "You've just come out of a coma. I'm not sure you're ready to be going anywhere."

"I've just spent the last year of my life in this bed. I think I deserve a break."

The doctor peered over his bifocals.

Lee eyeballed him with resolve.

"Fine, but you'll go in a wheelchair with one of my nurses."

That would work. Lee smiled. "Agreed."

****

The nurse pulled the double doors open and wheeled him inside. The altar sat vacant in front of a gold cross. She pushed him forward, the wooden floor creaking in defiance at every step. When they reached the front, he tried to step out of the chair, but his legs wobbled beneath him and he dropped to his knees, and folded his hands on the rust-colored cushions that likely held many tears.

"Are you okay," the nurse asked.

"I'm fine." He kept his eyes closed, searching for a way to reach God.

Lee wasn't sure he knew how to pray. His heart was heavy and his mind full. He figured he'd empty it all and allow God to do with it what he could. The last time Elena and he talked, she had been so angry. He loved her. He needed her.

Something dropped to his right. He lifted his head and wiped his eyes. A man bent to pick up a Bible from the floor in front of the first pew, obviously unaware of his presence. Lee watched him for a moment and then coughed.

The man looked toward him. "Oh sorry, I didn't see you there."

"Stan Heller?" Lee couldn't believe it.

Stan cocked his head to the side and stared. "Do we know each other?"

Lee motioned for the nurse to help him get back in the chair.

The nurse motioned to help him back in the wheelchair, but he waved her off. "Can I take you back now?"

"One second." He turned to Stan, "I'm Lee

Avarice. I witnessed one of your cases once."

"You're awake?" Stan shook his hand with mouth gaping open. "I don't know what to say."

Lee smiled.

"When did you wake up?"

Lee's head spun. He reached for the pew. The nurse stepped forward.

"Maybe you should sit down," Stan said.

"Yeah." Lee folded into the pew. His body felt weak, but his mind wasn't ready to retire again.

"This is so weird." Stan rubbed his face with both hands. "I came here to pray for you and now I wonder if I'm dreaming."

"A little faith, Stan. I think I know who killed your father."

"How could you?" The detective visibly swallowed. "I mean, how do you even know about him? You were in a coma before he was shot."

Lee chuckled. *Good question.* Whether he'd been dreaming, experiencing visions, or had been there, only God grasped why he knew. "He was shot by Melton."

"Yes, I know."

"You do?" Lee didn't expect that.

The detective took a seat in the second pew and leaned forward, folding his hands on the back of the pew. His eyes seemed moist and his expression drawn. "It's probably been one of the most exhausting experiences in my life. I feel like I know you, and yet this is the first time we've talked."

Lee sat across from him. He knew what the man meant.

"You were the key to all this, and I just thought you were a witness." Stan sighed. "Do you know who is responsible?"

"Krystal Heller."

Stan nodded and looked away. "Yes. My baby sister shot over a dozen men. Killed eleven."

"Is she...?" He couldn't finish his question. He feared the answer.

"She's in intensive care." Stan ran a hand through his hair and met Lee's eyes. "I'm sorry her rage affected you, but I'm glad you made it."

Lee felt remorse, but with an unusual sense of peace. "It is amazing how one mistake in our life can alter our future. Two lousy dice lost me my family, lost you your family, and almost lost me my life. It is I who am sorry."

Stan slid to the end of the bench and tilted his body to face Lee. "Krissy was who she was. She blames her problems on you, but she is responsible for her own actions. She's sick. I think my dad knew, but he didn't want to admit it." He bit his lip. "There were signs."

"Is she going to make it?"

"I don't know."

The nurse stepped forward. "I need to take you back."

"It was nice meeting you," Lee said.

Stan nodded. "You too."

The nurse wheeled Lee into a room on the third floor. "Here you go."

He looked around. The walls were a sunny yellow. Curtains, carpet, and wall hangings indicated he was in a different room than before. "This isn't my room."

"It is now. Since you're awake, we want you to enjoy your stay in a single suite." She pushed the metal footrests out of the way and placed her hand under his arm. "You should get back in bed."

He obeyed, but the room felt foreign. It was nicer, yes, but after a year in the other room, this felt odd. "May I make a phone call?"

"Dial nine." She nodded to the phone by his bed.

"Thanks."

The door closed behind him. He picked up the phone and punched in Elena's cell phone number.

"Hello?"

"Elena, don't hang up. We need to talk."

Chapter Thirty-Eight

Stan moved to his car, swallowing hard to hold back the bile that pushed against his throat. His hand trembled as he brought the mike to his mouth. He had to put out a shoot-to-kill APB on his own sister. How could he do this?

"Dispatch—"

There was a tap on his window.

He jumped. It was Kari. He rolled down his window. "Hi."

"Can I get in?"

"Please do."

She went around the vehicle and opened the door. A soft vanilla scent filled his car as she sat next to him. "I tried to get you inside, but I just missed you."

"Sorry, I'm a bit distracted. My sister got away."

"I heard." She turned sideways to face him and touched his hand. "Want to talk about it?"

He peered up to the roof to avoid crying in front of his girlfriend. He blinked away tears. He wanted to be mad. Bitter. But he couldn't. He loved his baby sister. He pictured her in her Easter dress so long ago. So innocent. So—

He sighed and grabbed hold of Kari's hand. "The hardest part is knowing who to hate."

"What do you mean?" she asked.

"I had this great talk with Lee and told him I

wasn't bitter. But the truth is, I'm swimming in emotion I can't even define. Do I hate Lee because he conned my sister? Do I hate Melton for shooting my dad? Or do I hate Krissy for shooting Lee, causing this whole ripple effect?"

"Maybe you don't hate anybody. Maybe you can forgive them all."

Stan squeezed his eyes shut. "Eleven people died! Almost a dozen innocent people died, just because my sister fell for some stupid dice game in high school."

Kari gasped. "Your sister shot eleven people?"

He opened his eyes and looked at her. "It's not clear how many people my sister killed. But we know for sure she shot Melton. The rest may have been a cover up."

"A cover up?"

"To get rid of witnesses, or to make it look like a serial killer to hide their tracks. Or in her words, revenge. Who knows? The stuff she rattled off in her to the cops was the voice of insanity."

"And you'll be investigating her?"

Tossing the radio mike from his lap, he said, "No, I'm done. Conflict of interest." He pulled Kari close and touched his mouth to hers. Soft and inviting, it felt like their first kiss. "I love you. I'm so sorry you got caught up in all of this."

She slowly opened her eyes and met his gaze. "It's because I'm so in love with you that I'm still here. And I will continue to be as long as you'll have me."

He touched her cheek. An amazing woman that understood more than she should. Stan always had a feeling he'd know when he met the perfect one. And he was right.

****

Elena arrived on a Monday to take Lee home. She wouldn't promise anything, and he couldn't blame her. After all he'd put her through, he was lucky she didn't pull the trigger first.

"You can stay in the guest room for now," she said, helping him to the couch.

"Thank you, Elena." He looked around their old home. She must have moved back in when she heard what happened. "Can I ask you a question?"

"I guess." She sat on an ottoman and removed her shoes.

"Why didn't you come visit me?"

She stared at him a moment before answering. "How do you know I didn't?"

"Did you?"

"Only once."

"One time in a year?" His heart sunk.

"Lee, it's complicated." She stood and walked into the kitchen, returning with two bottles of cranberry juice. She offered one to Lee and rested on the loveseat. "You brought out so many conflicting emotions in me. Anger, sadness, remorse, hatred..." She looked at him. "Love."

He leaned forward, but she recoiled deeper into the seat cushion. "I couldn't see you. It hurt too much. My heart took pity, but my mind was glad you were there. And then I felt guilty for even thinking such thoughts. You hurt me, and your coma took its toll."

Lee gulped. Shame fell heavy on his chest. A wall of skepticism and distrust lay in her eyes. He thought back to how he had changed things in the mirror. How he had tried to do right. He wished he had the same second chance now. "I'm so sorry, Elena. I never wanted to hurt you. If I could take it all back, I know I would have made different choices." He tried to ingest the painful emotion that sought to make him cry again. "I know it isn't fair to ask for a second chance, but if you give me one, I promise it will be different this time."

She stared at her hands, but didn't speak.

Silence without some sort of playful smile with Elena was never a good thing. In all the years he'd been married, she'd only been silent like that twice. Once when he'd disappointed her and second when she chose to leave him. Lee laid his head back. The couch seemed to sway beneath him.

"Some things take time, Lee." Elena stood. "But I'm not going anywhere."

Chapter Thirty-Nine

Stan kneeled at his father's grave with a plant in his hand. His father often laughed at the idea of a man bringing another man flowers. "A man's man wouldn't want daffodils," he would say.

With a smile, Stan placed the clay pot next to the marker bearing the Heller name. A cool breeze swept the leaves around his feet. The air felt thick. He touched a palm to the top of the stone, and sighed. "I'm sure you know what Krissy did. You wouldn't be here if you weren't such a good cop." His voice cracked. "They found her by our old house sitting in the backyard next to the dog house. But she's okay. They took her in."

Stan glanced over his shoulder where his fiancée waited in the car. "I wish you'd lived to meet Kari, Dad. You would have loved her almost as much as me." He stood and exhaled. "Whew. Well, I'd better go."

He touched the gold star embedded in the marble. "I love you, Dad. And I'll make sure my sister will be okay. I promise." He patted the marker one last time and walked toward the car. A great feeling of release fell over him. It was as if he had buried it all with his father and now he could live.

Kari stepped from the car. "Are you okay?"

He grabbed her and brought her lips to his. "Let's get married."

"I thought we were getting married."

He kissed her again. "No, I mean, let's set a date."
"You mean it?"
"With all my heart."

Chapter Forty

It took a few weeks for Lee to start feeling better, but eventually, he was able to get around without the desire to pass out. He watched every talk show he could stomach, bought too much on the home shopping network, finished every crossword in the house, and gained ten pounds through boredom snacking. He had to get out of here. *Where are the keys? Ah ha!* He grabbed them off the kitchen counter and started for the door.

Elena blocked his path with arms folded. "Where do you think you're going, mister?"

"Outside," he said, looking at the sunlit sky over her shoulder.

She shook her head. "Doctor's orders. You can't drive yet."

"But I'm tired of being cooped up here. If I watch one more soap, the world is going to see my stomach turn."

She didn't budge.

"Look, I need to take care of something."

"What?"

How he loved his stubborn wife. He knew better than to go into battle with her. His pellet gun of charm was no match for her tank of mulishness. Handing her the keys, he said, "You drive then."

****

"There, that's the one." Lee pointed to the complex on the left side of the street.

"Who lives here?"

It looked just as it had in the mirror. "Maybe no one. I just need to see." They climbed out of the car. He couldn't believe how familiar everything appeared. They climbed the steps to the second floor and knocked on the blue door. It opened, revealing a young Hispanic woman. "*¿Puedo ayudarle?*"

"Oh, I'm sorry. I must have the wrong house. I was looking for my aunt, Victoria Krueger."

"*Ella vivió aquí antes de mí.*"

"I'm sorry." He glanced at Elena, who shrugged. "*No habla Español.*"

The women pressed her lips together. "Ah..." She touched her chest. "Live here no more." She pointed down the stairs. "Landlord help."

Lee grinned. "Thanks."

"Your aunt?" Elena seemed surprised. "I didn't know you had any living relatives."

He glanced at her. "I may not."

The screen door to the manager's suite was half-open and a Whitney Houston song blared in the background. "Hello?" Fred looked around. The room had little furniture, and the few pieces scattered around the room looked as if they had been confiscated from a Dumpster. "Anyone here?"

A shadow appeared on the wall, and he turned around. A middle-aged woman dressed in a Hawaiian dress entered with a cigarette hanging out of her downturned mouth. "You need something?"

"I'm trying to track down my aunt, Victoria Krueger. I wondered if you have a forwarding address."

The woman took a long drag on her cigarette, keeping her eyes fixed on his. "She was taken to the convalescent home on Wilshire Street." She exhaled smoke and let out a raspy cough. "You know…the one that looks like a mansion."

He frowned. Yeah, he knew it. His aunt's health must be failing. "Thanks."

****

They pulled back out into traffic. "You know, I had a dream we had a daughter."

Elena didn't respond.

"We named her Rebecca. She was beautiful. Thick black hair. Blue eyes."

"I need to tell you something."

Something in the way she said that made his heart leap. "What?"

"I was pregnant when I left you."

"What?" He pivoted in his seat to face her. "We have a kid?"

She shook her head. "I miscarried when I heard you were shot."

Lee swallowed. The cars blurred outside the window. *Another casualty to my self-absorbed life.* "I'm sorry."

"That was another reason I didn't visit you. I blamed you."

"I understand."

She pulled over to the side of the road, placed the car in park, and faced him. "No, you don't. I don't blame you anymore. It wasn't your fault." She touched his face.

"How can you say that? Of course, it was."

"Look, the baby wasn't strong enough to make it.

258

God took him or her home. I'm done blaming you." She touched her fingers to his cheeks.

He grabbed her hand and kissed the back of it. "I know you wanted a family all along, but I was too selfish. I want to give you that now."

She raised an eyebrow. "You want kids?"

"If they'll be as beautiful as you, you bet." He smiled. "But first you have to let me back in your bed."

She swatted him playfully and sighed. "I think that could be arranged."

****

A gold sign bearing the words Prospect Convalescent Hospital marked the lawn in front of a three-story brick building. Elena found a spot near the front and walked around to his side. "You want me to get a wheelchair?"

Lee laughed. "No. They'll put me back in my room if you do."

"No, they'll put you back if you faint on the way in."

"I'll be fine." Walking up the driveway, he breathed in the fragrant smell. Violets and multi-colored tulips lined the path. A soft breeze caressed his face. He closed his eyes and inhaled again. Yes, freedom was a blessed thing. "I can't believe she might have been with me the whole time," he said, swinging open the glass door. The marble lobby was filled with old Victorian couches, thick tapestries, and Persian rugs.

"Did you provide for your aunt? This place must cost a fortune."

Lee opened his mouth to speak, when a woman behind the counter looked up and smiled. "Can I help you?"

"I'm here to see a family member."

She pulled off her bifocals and set her pen down. "Have you been here before?"

He glanced at Elena. "Yes, you could say that."

Elena turned away, hiding a smile.

"What's the name?"

"Victoria Krueger. She's my aunt."

The woman placed her glasses back on her nose and turned to her computer screen. She typed a few keys and then looked back at him. "She's in room 209, on the second floor."

"Thanks." He grabbed Elena's hand and walked to the elevator just off the lobby. They stepped out of the car on the second floor. The foyer was filled with more plush chairs and carpets. They moved down the hall to room two hundred and nine. He started to push the door open, but stopped.

"*Déjà vu*," he said aloud. A light flickered at the end of the hall. He wondered if that was his room from before.

"What?" Elena asked.

He started to walk toward the light when he heard his aunt's voice from inside the room. "Is somebody there?"

Lee glanced back at Elena. "Maybe I should go in alone."

She patted his shoulder. "Okay. I'll wait here."

He pushed the door open. His aunt sat on top of a crocheted blanket reading a novel. Her cheeks were hollow, but still had some color. "Hello, Auntie." Lee drug his feet like a kid in trouble. "It's me, Freddy."

She squinted. "Freddy?"

"Yes, it's me. How are you feeling?"

"Like a woman dying of cancer." She opened her arms and grinned with moist cheeks. "Come here, my boy. I can't believe it is you. I dreamt you would come for so long."

He knelt on the floor next to her and hugged her frail chest. Warm tears dropped from her eyes and mixed with his. He leaned back. "I'm so sorry I hurt you."

"I'm glad you've come." She dabbed her cheek with a corner of the sheet. "I've kept tabs on you over the years. You're quite a success."

He got up and sat in the chair next to the bed. "Yes, and it almost killed me."

"How are *you* feeling?"

"Better."

"I read about you being shot." She tried to sit up, but started coughing and pointed to a plastic cup by the bed. "Would you mind?"

He handed her the cup.

She sipped until her cup was empty. "I'm glad to see you're okay."

"If you knew where I was, why didn't you bring me home?"

Her eyes stared at him with a soft expression. "I wanted it to be your decision. You can't force love, son."

A tight feeling invaded his throat. She looked so tired. Regret cascaded over him. All those years... He wished he could have them back, have memories of spending time with this wonderful woman. "My wife is outside. Would you like to meet her?"

"I'd love to."

He stood up, glad for the distraction, and poked his head out the door. "Honey?" He waved.

She stepped around him into the room.

"Aunt Tori, this is Elena." He motioned from one to the other. "Elena, my mother's sister, Victoria."

Elena stepped forward and held her hand. Both women beamed. A rush of such joy overcame him that he almost shouted. He sat back and listened to the two women banter. After ten or so minutes of embarrassing stories, he decided to take a walk.

"Would you mind excusing me for a moment? I think I need to step out and allow my cheeks to cool down."

They both giggled. "He always did embarrass easily," Tori said.

"Go ahead. I'm dying to hear more." Elena smiled.

"I'm sure you are." He stepped out in the hall but not before hearing their laughter. His heart was so full, the joy overwhelming. He was glad they were getting along, despite that it was at his expense. He leaned against the wall and sighed.

A flickering light to his left caught his peripheral vision. He remembered it from when the door had been left open to his room. He had to go look. He squared his shoulders, cracked his knuckles, and stepped toward it. His shoes squeaked down the buffed hallway, making the journey a bit eerie. Fear overtook him and he turned away. *I'll enjoy life as it is. I've had enough treks to the past.*

"Are you lost?"

He turned around. *Kari Jensen?* He glanced up. "Hi."

Kari cocked her head sideways. "Do I know you?"

"Yeah," Lee said. "You were my nurse for a year."

She studied him for a moment. "Aw, yes, Mr. Avarice?"

"Lee, please."

A big smile crept over her pretty features. "I'm glad to see you're doing well." She brushed a piece of hair away from her face and the glimmer of a diamond ring caught his eye. "Have you and Detective Heller set a date yet?"

She raised an eyebrow.

"You know, your kindness doesn't go undetected when someone is in a coma. Thank you for always talking to me and taking such good care of me."

Without warning, she hugged him. He didn't know what to do, so he hugged her back. "I've always assumed that. Thank you for making my day." She pulled back. "And actually, Stan and I are getting married this Saturday. You should come." She smirked. "Since you got us together and all."

"I'd love too."

They stared at each other for a moment and then she pointed over her shoulder. "Were you going in there?"

"Yeah."

She seemed confused. "Really?"

He looked at the open door behind her. "Yeah, is that okay?"

"It's just that William Bentley hasn't had a visitor in over fifty years."

Lee's heart thumped. "Did you say, William?" *Could it be Bill? Bill is here?*

She scrunched her eyebrows. "Yeah? How could you know him?"

"Oh, um, my grandpa mentioned him."

She didn't look convinced, but seemed to wave it off. "I was just coming out to call the morgue to claim his body." She caught his gaze. "He passed away a few minutes ago."

Sorrow covered Lee like a scratchy blanket. "Can I see him?"

She offered him a half smile. "I guess." She stepped out of the way and motioned for him to enter.

Lee stepped forward. An empty bed sat to his right and a curtain lay in front of him. He pulled it back to reveal a sheet-draped body. He moved next to the bed and reached for the end of the white cloth. His hand shook. He grabbed the end and lifted it back. He gasped. A familiar ashen face rested peacefully on the pillow. It was indeed Bill. *My coma companion. My friend.* Saltwater cascaded down Lee's cheeks. Emotion he'd never felt before welled in his chest.

"I'm okay, Bill." He wiped at his face and knelt at the side of the bed. "I found the peace you spoke about." He grabbed Bill's hand and looked at his body again, but knew the shell was empty. Bill's soul had found the "bright light" and was now in Heaven.

Lee touched Bill's face with the palm of his hand. "Thank you."

Movement sounded behind him and he turned. Two orderlies stood in the doorway with a cart in tow.

"I'm sorry, sir," one orderly said. "But we need to take his body. Are you his next of kin?"

He shook his head and moved away.

They rolled the cart in the room and then proceeded to lift Bill onto the gurney. They placed the sheet back over his face and rolled him out the door.

Lee sat numb on the end of the second bed, which had been his for all that time. Hard to believe they had shared a room, and he didn't know. He looked around the room, amazed at how it all looked the same. The sunlight beamed off the mirror at the far end of the room. It had done its job.

"You know, William didn't have any relatives." Kari walked into the room. "It's nice to see someone here for him at the end."

"Do you know what put him in the hospital?"

"I wasn't here, of course, but according to Nurse Higgins, he was a wealthy entrepreneur right up there with the likes of John D. Rockefeller. I guess he gave it all up to become a missionary. Apparently, fifty years ago, he was building a shelter in Mexico, fell, hit his head, and slipped into a coma."

He shook his head. "Incredible."

"I can't imagine being in a coma for that long." She walked over to where Bill had slept for over five decades and touched the sheet. "I wonder what the mind must think about."

He beheld the room, envisioning his friend on the black stool in the corner. He smiled. "I'm sure he was entertained."

A word about the author…

Kimberlee works full-time as an adjunct professor and the Director of Instruction at San Diego Christian College. She is also a graphic designer for The Wild Rose Press, and a Creative Arts pastor for San Diego Hope Church. She resides in San Diego, CA with her husband and two teenage boys. Mendoza has her BA in Human Development, MA in Humanities, and is currently working on her Ph.D. in Leadership Studies in Education.

www.kimmendoza.com

Thank you for purchasing
this publication of The Wild Rose Press, Inc.

If you enjoyed the story, we would appreciate your
letting others know by leaving a review.

For other wonderful stories,
please visit our on-line bookstore at
www.thewildrosepress.com.

For questions or more information
contact us at
info@thewildrosepress.com.

The Wild Rose Press, Inc.
www.thewildrosepress.com

Stay current with The Wild Rose Press, Inc.

Like us on Facebook

https://www.facebook.com/TheWildRosePress

And Follow us on Twitter
https://twitter.com/WildRosePress